Golden & Grey

(An Unremarkable Boy and a Rather Remarkable Ghost)

LOUISE ARNOLD

Aladdin Paperbacks

New York   London   Toronto   Sydney

ALADDIN PAPERBACKS
An imprint of Simon & Schuster Children's Publishing Division
1230 Avenue of the Americas, New York, NY 10020
Copyright © 2005 by Louise Arnold
All rights reserved, including the right of reproduction
in whole or in part in any form.
ALADDIN PAPERBACKS and colophon are trademarks of
Simon & Schuster, Inc.
Also available in a Margaret K. McElderry Books hardcover edition.
Designed by Ann Zeak
The text of this book was set in Bembo.
Manufactured in the United States of America
First Aladdin Paperbacks edition May 2006
2 4 6 8 10 9 7 5 3 1
The Library of Congress has cataloged the hardcover edition as follows:
Arnold, Louise, 1979—
Golden and Grey (an unremarkable boy and a rather remarkable
ghost) / Louise Arnold.—1st ed.
p. cm.
Summary: When a downhearted ghost becomes the "invisible friend"
of an eleven-year-old boy who is an outcast in his new school, the
two help each other find their place in their respective worlds.
ISBN-13: 978-0-689-87473-4 (hc.)
ISBN-10: 0-689-87473-1 (hc.)
[1. Ghosts—Fiction. 2. Self-realization—Fiction. 3. Friendship—
Fiction. 4. Bullies—Fiction. 5. Schools—Fiction. 6. England—Fiction.]
I. Title.
PZ7.A73595Go 2005
[Fic]—dc22
2004020508
ISBN-13: 978-0-689-87585-4 (Aladdin pbk.)
ISBN-10: 0-689-87585-1 (Aladdin pbk.)

To Kieran, Ming, Dad, Matt, Rooskie,
and everybody who has helped me along the way

BOOK ONE

• • • • • • •

The Way Things Are

Grey Arthur

SOME GHOSTS ARE ALL LIGHTNING AND FIERCE EYES, chains rattling and dramatic wailing. Some ghosts are made of mischief and mayhem, rearranging furniture when backs are turned and laughing a silent laugh at shocked faces. Some ghosts are made of centuries of tears, and just seeing them makes you feel sad for weeks after. Some ghosts seem like normal people, just a more see-through shade of real. And some ghosts, ghosts like Grey Arthur, are made of cloud, with no firm edges, and aren't very ghostlike at all. Ghosts like Grey Arthur don't make you feel scared, or confused, or sad: Ghosts like Grey Arthur you tend not to notice at all.

Which, thought Grey Arthur, was decidedly unfair.

However, fair or not, this was the way it was, and this was the way it continued to be.

The centuries spun on, as the centuries do, night

following day following night. The seasons chased one another like a dog chases its tail—summer, autumn, winter, spring . . . The hours rolled forward, the world grew older, paths turned to streets, streets turned to roads, roads turned to motorways. Castles fell quiet, then fell into ruins, then buzzed and whirred into life once more, full of tourists and tea shops and books on local history.

The world was changing, and yet some things stayed the same. Humans ate and slept and worked, ghosts haunted, screamed, and were mischievous, and Grey Arthur . . . Well, he was Grey Arthur, and didn't really do much.

The corridors of time echoed with hauntings, with the sound of Chain Rattlers rattling, Screamers screaming, Sadness Summoners weeping, Poltergeists laughing . . . Stories around campfires, or sealed inside books, talked of the Faintly Reals, of Bugs, of Snorgles, of faces underneath your bed or objects moving with nobody nearby. Ghost stories etched into legends, made into films, guided tours to haunted locations . . .

There were no stories about Grey Arthur passed down through the years. No legends, no myths, no tales told in whispers at sleepovers, no costumes stitched for October 31. What stories are there to tell about a ghost who isn't scary? About a ghost who doesn't haunt? What stories are there to tell about a ghost who just tends to fade into the background?

All that was about to change, though.

Because this is where Grey Arthur's story begins.

(It's a story he shares with someone else, but we'll get to that later.)

Arthur's story doesn't begin with a Once Upon a Time, in a Land Far Away. It begins with a Tuesday, in England, on a bench in a park.

It begins with a cold, damp day. A day where the sky is dull with bloated clouds that threaten rain. A day where the sun has decided it has far better places to be than on the cold misty edges of England.

It begins with Grey Arthur, sitting on that bench with his head in his hands (not literally, like some ghosts do, but in the way that miserable people sit), watching the Real World go by. Watching humans walk dogs, and play soccer, and eat sandwiches, and do whatever humans do on a Tuesday. The humans couldn't see Arthur, as humans can't see ghosts, but even if they could have seen him it's very unlikely they'd have been scared. Confused maybe, a little bewildered, but there wouldn't be a hint of terror. Grey Arthur just simply didn't look scary.

The best way to honestly describe Grey Arthur is that he looked as if he had been put together in a hurry. When he remembered to have two ears, one was invariably a bit higher on his head than the other, and his hair seemed to have been designed for someone with a different-shaped head. He looked like a boy, and was little-boy shaped, but a boy who had been photographed with a shaky camera, and his outline was all blurred. He wore a little ghostly shirt and waistcoat, and little ghostly trousers, with ghostly socks that didn't match and ghostly shoes that were all scuffed. When Arthur's concentration wandered, he tended to fray around the edges and become more cloudlike than child shaped, and this annoyed him endlessly. Finally, to top it all off, Grey Arthur took his name from the fact that he looked like he was made in black and white, like the old movies were.

Grey Arthur, all untidy and put together in shades of grey, sat on a bench in England on a grey-skied day, feeling thoroughly sorry for himself. See, the real problem, the thing that caused the shadow of sadness to cling to Arthur, the thing that caused a heavy ball of misery to tug inside him, was that he hadn't found out what he was yet. There are more different types of ghost than there are different colors of crayon, and yet Grey Arthur didn't belong to any group. He wasn't scary enough to be a Screamer, wasn't naughty enough to be a Poltergeist, wasn't melancholy enough to be a Sadness Summoner . . . Each different thing Arthur had tried to be, he'd failed. So this is why, centuries of trying and failing later, Grey Arthur sat on a bench on his own, head in his hands, watching the world go by. That Tuesday was the day that Arthur had realized something, and it had made him feel even greyer than usual.

Arthur had realized that he'd never fit in. After all these endless years of trying, he realized that it was time to give up.

It began to rain.

"Life isn't fair." He sighed.

Tom Golden

TOM GOLDEN RUSHED THROUGH THE FRONT DOOR of number eleven, Aubergine Road, slamming it shut behind him, and hurtled straight up the stairs to his bedroom, slamming that door shut behind him too. He flung his schoolbag on his bed and sloped across to the mirror on the far wall.

"Tom, is that you?" shouted his mum from downstairs. "Tom, dinner's ready."

"I'm not hungry!" yelled back Tom. He peered into the mirror on his wall and saw his eye was beginning to turn slightly purple where someone's elbow had smashed into it. His bottom lip began to wobble. As he looked in the mirror, studying the bruising beginning to frame his eye, he noticed something pink in his hair. He reached up to pull it out, and as his fingers sank into it he realized it was bubble gum. Tom breathed deeply, biting back on tears. He tugged it as hard as he could, but the bubble gum simply stretched and pulled at his scalp, and wouldn't shift.

"Tom, honey, are you okay? It's your favorite dinner; it's bangers and mash. You sure you don't want any?" called his mum from downstairs again.

"I'm fine, Mum! I told you I'm not hungry!" Tom picked up a pair of scissors from his desk and carefully began to cut away the tangled-up hair. The chunk of bubble gum fell out, with patches of Tom's hair sticking out from it at angles. The remaining hair protruded from Tom's head, an embarrassing tuft. Tom tried sticking it down with some gel, but it refused to lie flat with the rest of his hair, determinedly sticking out at a funny angle. Sighing, he reached across and opened his clothes drawer, and after rummaging around he found a baseball cap and put it on. Sinking down onto his bed, Tom put his stereo on and breathed deeply, trying to keep the tears at bay.

The CD player whirred to life, and Tom's favorite band, Cold Fish, began singing their hit "Bottom Feeder." Tom turned up the volume. Sometimes, if you turned up the sound high enough, you could almost drown out your thoughts. Fill your head with guitar and drums and try to push out all the insults

that had been put there at school that day. Tom liked
that idea, but even with the music turned up so loud
that he could feel the bass rumbling in his chest, the
insults still whirred around his mind, like hamsters
running in a wheel, over and over and over again.

There was a knock at the door, and Tom turned the
volume back down again. It was Dad's knock. You
could always tell what parent it was by the way they
knocked. Mum knocked lightly and fast, whereas
Dad, by force of habit, always knocked out a little
tune. *Tap-tappy-tap-tap.*

"Are you all right, Tom? Mum said you're not feeling very hungry," Dad said through the door.

"I'm fine, Dad."

"Can I come in?"

"No, I'm getting changed," lied Tom.

"You're not ill, are you?"

"I'm fine, Dad."

"You sure?"

"I'm sure, Dad."

"Well, you know if you want to talk . . ." Dad
trailed off. Tom knew what he meant. "If you want to
talk, I'm here, Tom," is what he would say. Tom didn't
want to talk. What was there to say? What could Tom's
dad do? Move them back to where they used to live?
They'd only just finished unpacking here, the dustbin
still filled to breaking with broken-down cardboard

boxes and discarded bubble wrap. Make the kids here like him? If Dad intervened they'd make even more fun of him than they already did (if that was even possible). No, Tom didn't want to talk. . . .

"Honestly, Dad, I'm fine. Just a little tired, that's all." He paused, trying to make his voice sound as light as possible. "I'll be down in a bit."

Tom heard his dad's footsteps traipsing back down the stairs, and he sat up on his bed and began to get changed out of his school uniform. He took off his tie and threw it on the floor. As he took off his shirt, he realized the whole back of it had been flicked and sprayed with pen ink, and stuck slam in the middle was a little note that had been taped on at some stage of the day. FREAK, it read, in big, fat letters.

The strange thing was, Tom Golden was an incredibly normal boy. His hair (which fitted his head perfectly, apart from the new tuft where the bubble gum had been) was mousy brown, and his eyes were also brown, like chestnuts or melted chocolate. He had two ears, both the same height, and there was nothing peculiar about them. They weren't pointed, or tiny, or massive, or green. They were distinctly average human ears on a distinctly average head. He was slightly shorter than most of the other kids in his class, but he wasn't pocket sized, simply smaller than average sized, and there's nothing wrong with that. He was the youngest in his year, a side effect of having a birthday on August 31, something that probably didn't help the height gap between him and the rest of the children in his school. He didn't look like he had been made in a rush: Everything was where it belonged and nothing was blurred or faded about him. He was an only child, but there was nothing odd about that either, as many children are only children; and his parents were normal parents. They didn't lock him in a cellar and make him eat coal, and they didn't dress him in gold and spoil him rotten. They didn't make him eat broccoli if he hated it, and they didn't let him swear. They were normal parents, and Tom was a normal boy, except somehow he was weird, a freak, and very much different from everyone else.

It had to be true, because the other kids said so.

This note was final proof.

It hadn't been like this in his old school. In his old school Tom had always had somebody to talk to at lunchtime. In his old school he'd always had enough friends to fill a birthday party. In his old school he hadn't had bubble gum spat in his hair, or had elbows bruise his face. In his old school he hadn't been a freak.

But his old school, and his old friends, were miles and miles and miles away. Tom Golden had started secondary school in a place with no familiar faces, and certainly a distinct lack of friendly ones.

Tom crumpled up the note and threw it in the bin, and then threw his shirt in the general direction of the laundry basket. He sank back on the bed and stared up at the ceiling, tears starting to form as fast as he tried to blink them away. He turned the music back up, but even Cold Fish couldn't chase this sadness away. His eye throbbed with pain where the bruise was beginning to form. It was only Tuesday, which meant he still had all of Wednesday and Thursday and Friday to go before the weekend, and then only two days off before he had to start it all over again. The name-calling, the spitting, the notes, the laughing, the lonely walks home, and the lunchtimes hidden away in a distant corner of the field where nobody could steal your food or push you when the teachers weren't looking. The summer holidays seemed an eternity away. Tears ran down from Tom's eyes and dripped past his ears onto his bed.

Outside, it began to rain.

"Life isn't fair." He sighed.

Yesterday, and All the Days Before

THE GHOST WORLD SITS RIGHT ON TOP OF THE Real World, like butter sits on toast; the unreal world thinly spread over the real, overlapping at the edges. Ghosts walk down the same streets as humans, use the same buildings, even use the same lifts and sit on the same benches. The only difference is that humans, as a rule, can't see ghosts. You could sit next to a ghost on a bus or at the cinema and not even realize they were there. Some ghosts liked the fact that the humans couldn't see them. Some ghosts didn't care either way, and some ghosts wanted more than anything for someone to notice them sitting on a bench, or pulling scary faces, or peering in through a shop window and waving.

This is the way the world has been for hundreds and hundreds of years. Rumor had it that once the humans invented Science, they tried to explain everything they encountered. Why apples fall out of trees. Why the sea has tides. Why the sky is blue. When the humans got around to explaining ghosts, they drew a blank. Even the best scientists would scratch their heads and write sums and equations on scraps of paper before finally deciding that none of it made sense. They tried all kinds of experiments—seeing what would happen if a ghost fell out of a tree, what happens to the water in a bath if you add a ghost, what happens if a ghost flies a kite in stormy weather. None of the answers made a blind bit of sense, and it gave the scientists an awful headache (especially after one of the ghosts ate the kite, drank the bath water, and floated out of the tree). So they did what humans have been doing since the beginning of time, and will continue to do until the end of time, when they find a problem they can't explain or solve.

They ignored it.

Ghosts woke up one morning to find humans desperately pretending the ghosts didn't exist. The humans were rather good at it too. If a ghost tried to talk to a human, the human would simply hum really loudly or become strangely fascinated by the floor, or a wall, or they'd suddenly remember they left a lantern on, or forgot to tether the horse, and they would make a quick exit. Soon they were so fantastic at ignoring the ghosts that they didn't even have to try anymore. They genuinely couldn't see them. Any record of ghosts existing was suddenly dismissed as "stories," and that was that. The world made a lot more sense.

Time went on, as time always does. Ghosts could walk down the street, peering at humans straight in the face, and humans would have absolutely no idea they were there. Occasionally, ever so occasionally, rarer than blue moons and four-leaf clovers, a human would catch a glimpse of a ghost, and he or she would turn pale and point and make strange noises that weren't quite words, but as soon as the moment passed the person would do the typical human thing of trying to explain it all away. "Shadows . . . trick of the light . . . lack of sleep . . . too much coffee . . . not enough coffee . . . must have been the neighbor's cat . . ."

There were those who still vaguely believed in ghosts, even though they couldn't see them, those who read the old "stories" and thought that some might be true, but even these humans tried to find explanations for ghosts. They'd say they were memories caught in time, or the spirits of people who had died, or a premonition of something to come. Ghosts would chuckle at that. Ghosts are ghosts, as simple as gerbils are gerbils and seagulls are seagulls, and there's nothing to be explained. I haunt, therefore I am.

So this was the way the years churned on, the two worlds existing together and yet separate, like oil and water, or marbles and cream. That was, until something happened that caused those two worlds to collide together again. Something stronger than coincidence, and more flimsy than fate, something that hit both worlds at the same instant and, for the first time in too many years to remember, caused the Real World and the Ghost World to bump heads.

"Life isn't fair."

Now, it needs to be said that ghosts' ears don't really work like normal, Real ears do. Some ghosts don't even *have* ears, and those who do tend to have them only for display. Ghosts don't hear how loud or how quiet things are the way humans hear how loud or quiet things are: Ghosts hear things in a completely different way altogether.

Ghosts hear by emotion.

If you are really angry, or really sad, the quietest words can be the loudest screams to ghosts. If you've just had someone spill a drink all over your homework just after you've finished it, and you whisper, "Oh, pants!," while a human will barely hear you, a ghost will hear those words echoing around for hours, booming off the walls. Ghosts avoid sports days, people getting exam results, and long-lost family reunions, because they leave their heads ringing for weeks afterward. So when the human boy Tom Golden threw himself back on his bed, his eye tinged purple where an elbow had collided with it, a baseball cap hiding the tuft of hair that used to be a clump of bubble gum, his shirt sprayed with ink and a crumpled note calling him a freak lying in the bin, when that boy sighed, "Life isn't fair," those words roared through the Ghost World. They screamed through the air and hammered on walls, the length and breadth of the country. Every ghost in England heard (and even a few in France).

Grey Arthur, sitting alone on a park bench, watching the world go by, sighed, "Life isn't fair" and, at the exact same moment Tom's "LIFE ISN'T FAIR" bounced back at him, echoing along through the park, shaking the trees and tearing across the grass.

The words still rattled in Arthur's ears long after the actual shout had disappeared into the distance, and following that (not as loud as before, but still loud enough to make Arthur feel like his teeth were humming) came more shouted sighs about "NOT FITTING IN" and "BEING USELESS." Arthur slowly got to his feet, a lopsided smile spreading across his face. Ghosts have no time for coincidences, as they live in a world of magic, and omens, and portents, and signs, so this had to be something bigger, more important—Arthur had to find the source of this shouting. He left the bench, and the puddles beginning to form, and the people walking dogs and playing soccer and eating sandwiches and doing whatever humans do on a Tuesday, and he began to follow the shouting all the way back to its source.

Ghosts, being very light, and having no breath to run out of, can travel long distances very quickly, and Grey Arthur's little legs pounded along as he ran through England. The nearer he got to the sound of the shouting, the more his ears wobbled and his teeth chattered, so he knew he was going the right way. He darted through busy streets, past human shoppers who couldn't see him, past fields and farms, schools and motorways, his legs moving like a blur. Sometime he would pass ghosts in the street, or staring out of windows, holding their hands over their ears to block out the shouting (for all the good it would do them), and

Arthur would give them a little wave before pushing himself on. Drawing closer still, Arthur sprinted along winding roads and down dark alleyways that held strange cats and stranger smells, past skeletons of shopping trolleys and scattered remains of last night's take-away, past dogs that bark at gates and yards filled with plastic gnomes. Farther and farther he ran, little legs a flurry, until he finally found what he was looking for.

A row of normal-looking houses, stretching right and left. The road sign said AUBERGINE ROAD (although someone had helpfully written "SUCKS" after that in black marker). This was the place. It had to be: Arthur's hair was practically standing on end with the noise in the street. "WHAT IS WRONG WITH ME?" and "IT'S SO UNFAIR!" rattled up and down the road, and one house sat in the middle of all this clamor. The house looked as normal as every other house—a small yard with grass and a few flowers sat in front of it, and the door was painted a shiny green. The house was just like every other house, nothing different or odd, bar the fact it seemed to virtually wobble in the ground with all the emotional noise bursting from it. Any human walking up or down the street wouldn't notice anything strange, because human eyes are designed to see colors and shapes and read newspapers, not see sadness, but Grey Arthur could see the misery as clear as day. Arthur steeled himself and ran straight through the closed door of number eleven. (Much as Arthur hated running through objects, as it always made his head ache, this felt like an emergency.)

The noise was so loud here it actually made Arthur's teeth hurt, but he couldn't stop now. Two full-grown humans were chatting downstairs (something rather dull about bills and television licenses and the price of milk and just how long bangers and mash can stay warm for . . .), but they weren't who Arthur had come here to find. The noise was coming from above him, booming through the ceiling. He crept up the stairs.

At the top of the landing Grey Arthur found a door that had a poster on the outside. Drawn in different-colored felt pens, and with a skull and crossbones carefully sketched underneath, it read: KEEP OUT. BY ORDER OF TOM GOLDEN.

The door was nearly falling off its hinges with all the feelings being shouted on the other side. Arthur took another look at the sign and gulped. "It's too late now to turn back," he told himself, and he almost believed it too.

Arthur jumped through the door.

On the other side he found a human boy, eyes red and puffy from tears, and one eye slightly purple around the corners. Arthur remembered being told that humans are fragile, and change color if they are touched too hard, and so putting two and two together Arthur guessed that was what might have happened. The boy was still talking to himself, under his breath, and the sound was excruciatingly loud:

"AND I DON'T KNOW WHAT I'VE DONE TO DESERVE THIS, AND IT'S NOT MY FAULT I'M A FREAK, AND I DON'T SEE WHY THEY CAN'T JUST LEAVE ME ALONE, AND I WISH I WASN'T SO LONELY AND I WISH WE HADN'T HAD TO MOVE HERE AND I WISH I COULD FIT IN AND I WISH I HAD A FRIEND HERE AND—"

Grey Arthur looked at the human boy, Tom Golden, and everything just fell into place. He knew what he had to do. As a ghost, you're used to very little making sense, so when something finally *does* make sense you really shouldn't ignore it.

He was meant to find Tom.

You see, everyone needs someone who understands how they feel, and Tom was that person. They fitted together, like two pieces of a very easy jigsaw puzzle. Arthur was in need of something useful to do, Tom was in desperate need of a friend. How much simpler could this be? A decision was made, there and then, that seemed like the easiest thing in the world but that would turn out to be the biggest decision in Arthur's life.

Grey Arthur decided to become Tom's Invisible Friend.

Having never actually read the Terms and Conditions of becoming an Invisible Friend, nobody can really blame Grey Arthur for getting it wrong. It was an honest mistake, and honest mistakes are few and far between these days, with so many dishonest ones about. He was invisible, after all, and he did want to become Tom's best friend, so what more was there to it?

Nothing at all, thought Arthur. Okay, so ghosts can't touch humans. They'd never be able to high five, or play Thumb Wars, or plait each other's hair while giggling (or was that something only human girls did? So much to learn!) but surely that was only a tiny fragment of friend duties? Grey Arthur was superb at running through walls (which is a great bonus in hide-and-seek), he didn't get ill, so you wouldn't be able to catch chicken pox or mumps off of him, and he'd never borrow Tom's computer games and not return them, because most ghosts don't have PCs. The longer Arthur sat there and thought about it, the better the idea seemed. Sheer genius, in fact. The shouted whispers finally died away (which was just as well, as Arthur's head was thumping after jumping through two doors and his lopsided ears were still recovering from the earlier shouting) and Arthur set about his new job. *Invisible Friend.* It had a certain ring to it . . .

Soon Tom dried away his tears and did his best to look as if his eyes weren't red and purple. He put on a smile, and even though the smile didn't reach his eyes, he almost looked normal (as normal as humans ever look), and he wandered downstairs to get some food. As the door clicked shut behind him, Grey Arthur took the opportunity to set up home underneath Tom's bed. It was fairly cramped underneath there (mostly because every time Tom was told to tidy his room, he'd just throw everything under there to hide it, but partly because he refused to throw out the things he had apparently "outgrown" so they lived underneath the bed too). Arthur used a Pretty-Betsy doll as a pillow (Tom's aunt Sally had always sent him Christmas and birthday presents as if he were a girl) and a collection of old *Mr. Space Pirate* magazines as a duvet. Nestled underneath the bed, exhausted from a day of misery and surprises and running and ear-rattling noises, Arthur began to feel sleepy, and as he curled up with his head on the makeshift pillow he smiled to himself.

Tomorrow was going to be a big day.

Tomorrow was Arthur's first day in his new job as an Invisible Friend.

A New Day

WEDNESDAY STARTED THE SAME AS EVERY OTHER school day before it. The alarm beeped to life, and Tom groggily reached out and turned it to snooze. Five minutes later the alarm went off again, and Tom reached out and turned it off again. This battle, boy versus alarm clock, was fought every morning.

The alarm clock always won, even if sometimes it did get a little help from Tom's mum.

"Come on, lazybones, out of bed." Tom's mum strode into the room and pulled open the curtains, letting light stream into the room. Tom winced and rolled over, pretending to still be asleep. "No, you don't. Come on, out of bed." Tom sighed and sat up, and his mum smiled, the patient morning smile she wore at this same time every day. That smile suddenly froze, though, and she looked at Tom's face, concerned.

"What happened to your eye?" she asked. "I didn't notice that last night. How'd that happen?" She leaned over to look closer, and Tom pulled away and began packing his schoolbag.

"I got caught in the face with a cricket ball in PE," lied Tom. "It's all right, Mum, it doesn't hurt."

"A cricket ball? Ouch." She ruffled his hair, as mothers tend to do, and then realized one patch of hair was sticking out at a funny angle. "Did you do that to your hair?"

"Yes. Everyone else at school has got one too, Mum," lied Tom again. Parents believe kids will do anything if it's trendy, and Tom's mum was no different. She just looked at him as if he were crazy and shook her head, smiling.

"Well, I think it looks strange, but I suppose if you like it, that's the main thing." She waited to make sure Tom was out of bed and then left him to get ready. "Breakfast is on the table, okay, Tom?"

Tom wandered downstairs sometime after that, his shirt buttons done up wrong (not that he knew) and his school tie slightly lopsided, and sat down for breakfast. Dad was busy burning toast while doing up his tie and simultaneously trying out his latest product. Dad worked for Svelte Socks (The Socks That Say Style with a Smile!). The promotion that had forced the Golden family to move house in the summer holidays had changed Dad from being a normal manager to being "Manager in Charge of Designing New Socks"—not his official title, of course, but the official title was long-winded and dull. The new socks he was currently testing were Golden's Anti-Static-Shock-Sock (try saying that three times fast). Dad was frantically moonwalking on the carpet before touching metal objects to test the socks out, in between eating mouthfuls of burnt toast. It seemed the socks didn't

24

work all that well, though, as every now and then breakfast was punctuated by a loud "Ouch!"

Mum was also rushing to get ready for work. After moving, she'd managed to get a job at Thorblefort Castle, selling tea and crumpets and the occasional cheese and onion sandwich in "Ye Olde Tea Shoppe." It was a nice, quiet job, and the uniform wasn't too offensive. Every now and then Mum brought home all the leftover crumpets too, which was an added bonus.

Tom grabbed a slice of toast and a glass of milk. Mum had left Chuckle Choc-O Chunks cereal and Mr. Space Pirate Hoops on the table for him, but Tom felt he was far too old for cartoony cereal these days. He was eleven years old, and he was convinced that eleven-year-olds ate toast, and not breakfast cereal shaped like mini-spaceships or chunks of chuckle. Well, at least not on weekdays. So Tom ate some toast, Dad kept on touching the door handle to see if he'd get sparks, and Mum flapped around the kitchen getting ready. Wednesday morning was just another very normal school morning.

(Except for maybe a few small differences . . . Namely the fact that an invisible ghost was living underneath Tom's bed and had decided to be his best friend—something Tom had absolutely no idea about—and that this ghost was now sitting at the breakfast table staring in awe at the range of breakfast cereals scattered all over the tablecloth. Ghosts don't have breakfast, and so this was all very new to Grey Arthur, who was busy wondering if Mr. Space Pirate Hoops actually tasted of Space Pirate. . . .)

So, thinking this Wednesday was a very normal Wednesday, Tom wolfed down his toast, grabbed his packed lunch, threw it into his rucksack, and headed off to school with a ghost in tow.

As Arthur followed Tom on the way to school, he noticed small changes taking place. The cheeky grin that Tom had worn for his parents as he dashed out the front door faded the farther he walked, and he slowed down and dragged his feet, scuffing his shoes on the pavement. His shoulders slumped, and he seemed to grow smaller (and he was quite small to start with). He stared at the pavement the whole time he walked, head down, and thrust his hands deep into his pockets. As the tall walls of the school loomed in the distance, Tom actually ground to a halt. He stared at the entrance, trying to muster up his courage. He took two deep breaths, shook his head as if trying to shake away his nerves, and then forced himself on. Arthur followed behind Tom, peering over his shoulder at the huge cast-iron gates. Arthur felt nervous about his first day at school, which was faintly ludicrous, since Arthur had seen castles so haunted that you couldn't take two steps without stepping in a puddle of ectoplasm or tripping over some chains being rattled by a haughty-looking ghost, so going to school should be a piece of cake. It didn't feel like a piece of cake, though. There was something about the slow walk to those imposing gates that made Grey Arthur's hair stand on end.

WELCOME TO THORBLETON SECONDARY SCHOOL read the sign over the entrance. It didn't look particularly welcoming. Foreboding, perhaps. Ominous. Heavy black letters on a serious-looking sign.

Tom and Arthur stepped through the gates and into the world of the school beyond.

Almost instantly Arthur was immersed in noise. It slammed into him and made him wobble on his feet. A human equivalent would be when you have been swimming underwater and then come up to the surface, and all the sounds rush back into your ears, but multiply that by a hundred and you still wouldn't even be close. Arthur had never been near so many humans all in one place before, and young humans are umpteen times more noisy than full-grown humans, so it came as quite a shock. Grey Arthur's first instinct was to turn and run back out of those gates again, but seeing how glum and small Tom looked, he knew he had to stay. A good friend wouldn't run away and leave his friend alone.

Tom sighed and muttered to himself as he slowly trundled through the school. Being new to the area, he'd not even heard of Thorbleton Secondary School before he'd turned up on the first day of term, after the summer holidays had dwindled to an end. Still, being held captive there from 8:25 to 2:50 every day, Tom had quickly learned the myths, the facts, the fables, and the legends of Thorbleton Secondary School.

Thorbleton Secondary School: A Beginner's Guide

THORBLETON SECONDARY SCHOOL WAS UNIFORMLY grey, a mass of concrete plonked unceremoniously on the edges of a school playing field, with a couple of disheveled-looking bike sheds separating the two. The school's motto, which was printed on a sign over the entrance to the school foyer, was "Cognito Ergo Sum," which the teachers took great delight in telling people was Latin for "I think, therefore I am." Once a month, however, regular as clockwork, someone would get a spray can of paint and change the motto overnight to "Cognito Ergo Bum." It would stay like that for a few hours the next morning until one of the teachers noticed all the pupils giggling, and then for the rest of the day Mr. Dean, the caretaker, would be stuck up a ladder armed with cleaning fluids and a frown (and muttering things that would get any pupil pulled in front of the Headmaster for saying) while he tried to restore the sign to its former glory.

The playing field was rapidly shrinking, as every few years they sold off a bit more land for people to build houses on, and so now the area looked a bit cramped as it tried to fit a soccer field, rounders field, cricket field, rugby field, and an athletics track on half as much space as it used to have. The long jump pit now doubled up as a handy pooing pit for the cats that had moved in with humans to the new houses, which was an added incentive for kids to try to jump as far as possible in the hope of clearing the sand altogether. No one had yet managed it, and so the person "volunteered" to do the long jump on school Sports Day was always the least popular person in the class.

Tom had a sneaking suspicion he'd be long-jumping on Sports Day.

As Tom wandered around the school, Grey Arthur followed him, eyes wide, taking in the strangeness of it all. Arthur had seen hundreds of years of history, seen the strangest fashions, seen plague and war and all things in-between, seen ghosts that would wear their faces inside out for the fun of it, but he'd never ever, in all his ghostly years, seen anything quite like the boys' toilet.

The ceiling in the boys' toilet was comprised entirely of once-soggy tissue that had been thrown up there and then left to dry to form toilet-paper stalactites, so the room had begun to look like a bizarre cave. That is, if caves were made of cheap abrasive pink toilet paper, which any geography teacher will tell you they are not. But if they were, this is very much how they would look. Graffiti appeared on the toilet doors as fast as Mr. Dean, the caretaker, could clean it off, and the room always smelled of strong bleach with a hint of, well, *boys' toilet*. Arthur walked timidly, afraid that the ceiling would come plummeting down at any second. He was sure the sensation of old dried toilet paper falling through him to the ground would be most unpleasant. Tom didn't even seem to notice the spiky pink ceiling that hung above him. He had other things on his mind.

As weird as the school was, as strange and insane and downright odd as the school was to Arthur, he did his best to pay attention. It was very important that, as a friend, he understand how Tom's world worked. So he watched, and he followed, and he made mental notes, and every minute Arthur learned something new about the strange, *strange* world of schools.

Lockers. Each human child had his or her own locker, which would invariably reek of smelly trainers and forgotten packed lunches that now had grown moldy. The inside of the locker would be plastered in half-peeled-off stickers where the pupil who had the locker before had had a crush on some boy band, and no matter how hard the new owner tried to remove the I LOVE BOBBY stickers, he or she always failed. Tom's locker had a particularly bad infestation of old boy-band stickers, noted Arthur. Half-torn faces stared accusingly back at Tom as he retrieved his science books or stashed away his PE gear, and he blushed if anyone was near enough to notice. The lockers were all dented or scratched, and some appeared to have been crowbarred open at the bottom, the metal doors bent permanently open at improbable angles.

Corridors. Apparently a means for getting from one location to another, corridors were places of astounding stillness during lesson times, and the location of avalanches of cascading humans with places to be for the five minutes between lessons. This alternation between emptiness and chaos was broken only by lunch breaks, which saw human groups standing at predesignated locations, in predesignated groups, and talking extremely loudly while dropping litter. As far as Grey Arthur could tell, Tom didn't have a predesignated location. Nor a predesignated group. Tom wandered on his own during these breaks.

Ghost schools and human schools are very different, thought Grey Arthur as he followed Tom through the corridors of Thorbleton Secondary. Ghost schools generally consisted of a few ghosts meeting in a very ghostly surrounding, like a castle or a sewer or a windswept cliff, and trying out new haunting skills, such as how to gargle fog or how to make ectoplasm in three easy steps. This human school was positively flooded with children bustling in the corridors, hanging around in doorways, queuing in toilets, and it was so loud with emotions that Arthur was worried his ears might actually drop off.

"OH NO, I FORGOT MY HOMEWORK!"

"MY TEACHER HATES ME, I'M SURE SHE HATES ME. . . ."

"OH MY, THERE'S MICHAEL, HE'S LOOKING AT ME, OH WOW, HE'S LOOKING AT ME!"

And as Arthur scurried after Tom, trying to block all the other voices out of his head, he could hear Tom shouting under his breath too:

"PLEASE LET TODAY BE BETTER."

Arthur was determined to make sure it would be.

And if Arthur was finding it very hard to get used to this school, well, so was Tom. The difference between junior school and secondary school is very marked indeed and takes a long time to get used to. Firstly, instead of staying in the same classroom all day, in this school you actually had to march around from room to room. Surely it would have made more sense for the teachers to come to them, rather than the other way round, especially as the teachers knew the layout of the school, whereas Tom spent much of his life horribly lost. Another thing Tom had learned, very much the hard way, was to beware whatever lurked underneath the desks. On his first day he'd pushed his knees up underneath the table and had found his trousers stuck there, glued by old chewing gum. Older children, twice the height of anything he'd seen in his old school, marauded through the corridors, and you quickly learned to get out of their way. And all the books! Tom had never been given so many books in all his life, and the seams of his schoolbag strained under the weight.

It was a strange new world for both boy and ghost.

Tom's first lesson was English, and Arthur sat cross-legged on the floor next to Tom's desk. The teacher was a very pointy woman, who seemed to be made entirely of sharp angles, and she wrote her name, Mrs. Lemon, in chalk on the blackboard. The chalk screeched as she dragged it into words. Her face was drawn into an unimpressed pout, and Arthur thought she was nearly as scary as anything you'd find rattling chains in a castle.

"Right, class," she hollered, her eyes scanning the room. "Pens and paper out now, you're going to take some notes. And no talking!"

Tom began rummaging in his bag, and his heart sank when he realized he'd forgotten his pencil case. "Oh, no, no, no," he muttered quietly as he desperately checked all the zip sections of his bag. "Please, please, please don't say I've forgotten my pen. . . ." Four pence in pennies, a packet of chewing gum, a novelty pencil sharpener, and an old bus ticket, but no pen . . .

Grey Arthur's ears twitched as he listened to Tom muttering, and he grinned. An opportunity to try out his new Invisible Friend skills! Arthur leaned across to the next desk. The child sitting there was busy picking his nose and staring into space, and so he didn't notice at all when Arthur plucked the pen off his desk (which is just as well, as a floating pen might have caused some alarm). Arthur gently placed the pen on Tom's desk. This Invisible Friend lark was quite easy after all. . . .

Tom finally stopped searching his bag and was just about to put his hand up to confess that he'd forgotten his pencil case when he realized that a pen had been on his desk all along.

I must be cracking up! he thought to himself with a relieved grin. A few seconds later he was really glad that he did have his pen after all, because when Pick-Nose Peter at the desk next to him put his hand up to say his pen had gone missing, Mrs. Lemon screamed at him until Tom thought one of her eyes would pop out.

Today was going better for Tom after all.

As the bell rang, and all the children pushed their way out of the class, Arthur faced his next challenge as an Invisible Friend.

A huge child, towering head and shoulders above the rest, barged through the door roughly, pushing

Tom to one side. His dark hair was cut short, as short as the teachers would allow without you getting suspended until it grew back, and his face was fixed into a permanent snarl. He locked eyes with any other child who dared look at him, and the other child would always look away first. His eyes were cold, and shallow, and dark like the sky before a storm. *Big Ben.* That was his name. He'd even written it across the knuckles of both his hands, to help you remember. He fixed his glare on Tom.

"Nice hair, freak boy," he spat. Tom self-consciously raised a hand to his hair, trying to smooth down the tuft. "And don't look at me like that, or I'll give you a second black eye to match the one I gave you yesterday." That was said loudly, so the other kids would know it was his handiwork bruising Tom's face. That was important to Big Ben. Tom quickly looked at the floor. "Better," said Big Ben.

Poor Tom was terrified: Arthur could sense fear surrounding Tom like coldness surrounds ice. An audience was gathering, kids from Tom's class and from passing classes circling around Tom and Big Ben, watching to see what would happen. Arthur looked back at Mrs. Lemon, but she was putting away books in the cupboard at the back of the room, oblivious to what was going on. Big Ben seemed to grow as the crowd grew, stronger, taller, louder.

"You look at me like that again, and I'll smash

your face in," he snarled, reveling in the hushed audience that had formed.

"I'm sorry," muttered Tom, staring at the floor.

"You what?"

"I'm sorry!"

"Not good enough. Why should I care if you're sorry or not? I don't even want a freak like you talking to me. You look at me again, I'll break your teeth." Big Ben stepped right up against Tom, toe to toe. The crowd watched silently, waiting for something to happen. Tom shut his eyes, and bit his lip, and held his breath. "What, you not gonna say anything? Come on, freak boy. Say something." He shoved Tom's shoulder, pushing him backward. "Say something! I dare you. Come on!" He shoved Tom again, harder.

Nobody ever agrees on what happened next. Some people say Tom must have thrown it, some say Big Ben must have, and some people say there was nobody actually in the class at the time and that it's a big mystery, but *somebody* picked a pen up from a desk in the classroom and sent it flying at Mrs. Lemon in the stationery cupboard. It hit her square on the back of the head before bouncing to the floor, and as she spun round angrily to shout at whoever had thrown the offending pen she noticed the crowd in the corridor. She bowled toward the door, a flurry of high-pitched telling-offs and gesturing hands, and the crowd quickly disappeared.

"This ain't over," hissed Ben, as he was herded away.

Suddenly the corridor was empty, as quickly as that. Just Tom and Mrs. Lemon remained.

"Tim, isn't it?" Mrs. Lemon asked.

"Tom, Miss."

"Tom, right. Are you all right, Tom? What was happening?"

"Nothing, Miss." Tom was still staring at the floor, hands in pockets to hide the fact that they were shaking. "We were just talking."

Mrs. Lemon "hmm"ed. It was the type of "hmm" noise adults make when they don't believe you but know they can't prove otherwise.

"Well, if you want to talk . . ." She trailed off into silence, and tried her best to smile reassuringly. Reassuring smiles didn't suit Mrs. Lemon's face, and it looked more like she'd bitten something acidic. Anyway, Tom didn't want to talk. What use would talking do? He shook his head, and wandered off to second lesson with his ghost in tow. A ghost who knew quite well who had thrown that pen . . .

Tom and Arthur trudged around with each other for the rest of the day, and Arthur did his best to live up to his job title. At lunchtime, a scrawny kid who smelled of ham had crept up behind Tom and stuck a sticker on his back that read FREAK BOY HAS TUFTY HAIR, and Arthur had carefully peeled it off without

Tom even knowing it had ever been there. Tom had no idea someone was sitting next to him as he ate his lunch. There is no loneliness in the whole wide world quite so deep and utterly miserable as the loneliness you feel when all around you are smiling faces, laughter, and people, and usually those long, lonely lunches were the most miserable times of all. Today, though, was different. Although Tom thought he was still all alone, today it didn't bite so deeply. Today was going better after all. Okay, so Big Ben had squared up to him, but he hadn't actually touched him, and Big Ben wasn't in every class he had (Big Ben rarely stayed in school for a full day anyway, having far more important things to do, like write his name on walls or smoke cigarettes). There had been no nasty notes all day. Maybe things would get better? Maybe it would just take a while for him to settle into this new school? Maybe things weren't so bad after all.

That day Arthur peeled four stickers off of Tom's back in total, took two notes out of his bag that had been put in there, and managed to get Tom's apple back to him after some kids stole it when Tom wasn't looking and hid it under a pile of books. Arthur took it back and put it in Tom's lunchbox before he'd even noticed it had gone. Grey Arthur was feeling particularly proud of his efforts as an Invisible Friend, and everything was going really well—he'd even begun to grow used to the terrible racket that human children make. As the rest of the day passed uneventfully, Tom had started smiling properly too, not the pretend smile that he did for his parents to convince them he was okay but a real smile, and that made Arthur grin too.

The last lesson changed things slightly.

As Arthur followed Tom into the final lesson of history—which was Tom's favorite lesson, taught by Mr. Hammond, Tom's favorite teacher—something very strange and completely unexpected happened.

Someone recognized Arthur.

"Arthur! Grey Arthur! Yooo-hooo! Arthur!" yelled Ballpoint Bill, who was perched in the corner of the room, chewing on a pen that was currently leaking ink all down the side of his mouth. Bill was waving enthusiastically, his pudgy arms wobbling. Tom walked over to sit at his desk, oblivious, and a rather shocked Grey Arthur wandered over to where Bill was sitting. Ballpoint Bill and Arthur had met nearly fifty years ago, when Arthur had trained to be a Poltergeist— Arthur had failed the class awfully, and Ballpoint Bill hadn't done much better. He'd managed to pass, but by the flimsiest of margins.

Poltergeists are renowned as the most mischievous ghosts of all, and they spend most of their time moving and hiding objects from poor unsuspecting humans. Here is a little-known fact: *Poltergeist activity is responsible for ninety percent of all cases of losing a sock in England.* Young Poltergeists start off by stealing socks, in order to make the remaining one "odd," then progress to hiding house keys, and similar acts of naughtiness, eventually working up to greater levels of mischief as they get older and stronger, before finally specializing in a field of expertise. Quite often you'll find Poltergeist gangs in supermarket car parks, shuffling the cars and then laughing until they fall over at all the humans trying to remember where they parked. Legend even has it that one day in 1997, when a human called Mr. Whistle was running late for a job interview, a Poltergeist by the name of the Red Rascal managed to hide an entire building! No human ever believed Mr. Whistle that the building had gone missing, and so he didn't get the job, but the ghosts all knew the truth.

Arthur had never been very good at stealing socks. To be honest, he'd always felt a bit mean taking something that didn't belong to him, and that was why he had failed—he was caught sneaking back into a bedroom in the early hours of the morning returning enough odd socks to outfit a one-legged rugby squad. The Poltergeist teachers had not approved of this distinctly un-Poltergeisty behavior, and Arthur had failed the course. Ballpoint Bill, on the other hand, had no problem at all with taking things that didn't belong to him—his problem was that he was lazy, and a bit of an underachiever. Even stealing socks was too much like hard work. Ballpoint Bill got his name from his

Poltergeist specialty—stealing pen caps and all things inky. The other Poltergeists weren't particularly impressed, but Ballpoint Bill seemed happy, and that was the main thing.

"Bill!" said Arthur, genuinely surprised to bump into him here. "Still stealing pen caps?" Bill grinned, and Arthur saw that his pockets were brimming with chewed pen tops, and the occasional entire pen. Splotches of ink stained all of Bill's patchwork colors, from years upon years of stealing pens and chewing them, and even more years of not washing. Even Bill's teeth were blue and black.

"You know me, Arthur, always after the easy life." Bill reached into his pocket and brought out some ink cartridges, and he popped one into his mouth and began to chew it thoughtfully. He offered Arthur one, but Arthur declined. "What about you, Arthur, managed to find yourself a job yet?"

"Actually, yes, yes I have," said Arthur, a proud smile forming. Behind Arthur, the history teacher Mr. Hammond walked in, and even though there was no way he could hear the two ghosts having a conversation in his lesson, Arthur found himself beginning to whisper anyway. "I've become an Invisible Friend!"

Mr. Hammond got out the register and began calling names.

"An Invisible Friend? Never heard of them,"

sniffed Bill, popping another ink cartridge into his mouth. "What've you actually got to do, then?"

"See that human in the corner? The one with the brown hair?"

"And the silly tuft?" asked Bill.

"That's the one." Arthur nodded. "Well, I'm his Invisible Friend. I follow him around, and I help him out, make sure he isn't lonely, and look after him and try to make it so nothing goes wrong for him."

"You just made that job up!"

"No, I didn't. I'm sure I read about it somewhere. Besides, I'm rather good at it. Earlier on I even managed to stop him from getting hurt by another large human child, which isn't bad for my first day! Look—see! He's smiling." Bill and Arthur took a second to study Tom, and sure enough, he was smiling. He looked genuinely happy, and that made Arthur grin even more. "See, one happy human!"

Mr. Hammond called out Tom's name.

"Tom Golden?"

"Yes, Dad," replied Tom.

Dad.

The class erupted first into fits of giggles, then all-out laughter, and the smile drained right from Tom's face. Even the corners of Mr. Hammond's mouth twitched as he struggled to suppress a grin. Tom was turning crimson, and there was absolutely nothing Arthur could do. All day spent hiding notes, collecting pens, retrieving apples, and then this happened and all Arthur could do was watch poor Tom turn redder and redder.

"Oh well," said Ballpoint Bill, flicking another ink cartridge into his mouth, chewing noisily. "You win some, you lose some, I suppose, Arthur."

Tom wanted to leave the class as soon as humanly possible, and when the bell rang he practically leaped from his chair and flung himself toward the door. It wasn't to be, though. Mr. Hammond was waiting by the door, and every pupil had to file past him one by one and collect a consent form.

"We're going on a trip to the local castle, Thorblefort Castle, in a couple of weeks' time to get a sense of local history."

Thorblefort Castle? The place where Mum works? *Great,* thought Tom, *another opportunity to get horribly embarrassed.* Visions of his mum clutching scones and waving wildly at him in front of all the class immediately popped to mind.

"Don't forget to get the forms signed and back to me as soon as possible," announced Mr. Hammond as he handed out the slips of paper. Tom's cheeks burned hotly as he took the form and put it into his bag. Mr. Hammond smiled encouragingly at Tom, and that just made Tom burn redder.

"Don't worry about it, Tom," whispered Mr. Hammond as Tom hurried past. "They'll soon forget all about it."

Shows how much you know, thought Tom. As if it wasn't bad enough being Freak Boy, now he was Dad Boy as well, and children don't just forget things like that. "Dad" would be remembered *forever.*

Or at least a couple of weeks.

As Tom rushed home after last lesson, Arthur scurried after him, and he had time to reflect on the day. Okay, so maybe things hadn't been perfect, and maybe Tom had called his teacher Dad and there was nothing a friend, Invisible or otherwise, could do about that, but other than that it had been a good day. For the first time in his life, Grey Arthur had found something he was good at, and he wasn't ready to give up yet. And tomorrow he'd be able to try harder, and the day after that, until he became the best Invisible Friend that world had ever *not* seen.

Tom Golden and Grey Arthur: best friends.

Arthur liked the sound of that.

Meetings in Moonlight

THAT NIGHT TOM FELL ASLEEP FACE-FIRST IN A BOOK he was reading (some story about a boy with a scar and a magic stick, as far as Arthur could make out) and so Arthur gently pried the book out from underneath his face and turned out the bedside light. Tom muttered sleepily but didn't wake up. Arthur pulled the covers up to make sure Tom didn't get too cold, and when he was sure his friend was completely, utterly, one hundred percent asleep, Arthur sank through the floor to downstairs.

Tom's mum and dad were curled up on the settee together, watching a TV program where a presenter asks people questions, and if the people get them wrong they look all sad, and then the presenter tells them the correct answers. (Arthur decided this was rather mean, and that perhaps the people could use some Invisible Friends too. If the presenter knew the answers anyway, then why did she need to ask the questions in the first place? It just looked like bullying to him.) Leaving the parents to their television show, Arthur leaped through the front door and out into the night.

It was a clear night, and the full moon hung bright and low in the sky, framed by millions of stars. The seasons balanced halfway between summer and autumn, and the trees boasted colors that were beautiful in the day, but muted grey in the night. Grey Arthur felt more at home at night, when everything had its color dusty and faded, not just him. With the sun down, all the heat had fled with it, and the night had a chilly bite to it. Arthur didn't feel it, though. Being a ghost, he didn't get affected by the cold or the heat, and was still dressed as he was always dressed, whether it was summer or winter, rain or shine. It was a lovely night, a beautiful night, but Arthur didn't have time to stop and count the stars—there was someone he wanted to see.

Arthur began to run, out of Aubergine Road, past fish-and-chip shops, past bus shelters, down winding side roads and through countryside and fields. Faster and faster he ran, his little waistcoat flapping. Onward still, darting past people walking dogs, past men with red faces and redder noses who sang loudly and out of tune, past taxi ranks and kebab shops and cinemas, until he arrived at A Very Specific Old Chestnut Tree by an old city wall. Sitting underneath the tree, quill in hand, scrawling poetry on a sheet of paper by the moonlight, was Woeful William.

Woeful William was a Sadness Summoner and one of Arthur's oldest friends. When William spoke it sounded like it was raining inside your head. Centuries of being the most melancholy of ghosts had changed him from a dusty grey to the most depressing shade of blue, like the sky on a cold morning when everyone had forgotten your birthday. When William sighed, all the humans who couldn't even see or hear William sighed too. Just being near William could do that to you. William would sit in very dramatic places, like beneath weeping willow trees or in the grounds of old buildings, and recite poetry about the loneliness of life while waving a handkerchief and sighing very pointedly. People would walk past and then suddenly pause where they were. Their chins would wobble, and their hearts would sink, and they'd walk on a little sadder than before without ever knowing why. That was the very essence of being a Sadness Summoner.

Arthur and William had met centuries before, when Arthur had tried to become a Sadness Summoner. It had been, by all accounts, a bit of a disaster. Arthur's attempt at depressing poetry had ended up surprisingly upbeat ("There was a fluffy rabbit called Ian," it began), and no matter how hard William tried to coax Arthur into a miserable ending, the rabbit always lived happily ever after. Arthur also had a terrible habit of giggling if he tried to look serious for too long, and Sadness Summoners simply Do Not Giggle. Eventually, William broke it gently to Arthur that he really wasn't meant to be a Sadness Summoner, but they had decided to stay friends. William would test out his poetry on Arthur, and Arthur, well, he just enjoyed the company, really.

Tonight was a full-moon night, and every full-moon night you could find Woeful William in the same spot, underneath A Very Specific Old Chestnut Tree, bathed in the silver light and writing poetry.

William was predictable like that. Every half-moon you would find William at the old harbor in Bosham, staring out to sea, pondering the meaning of life (and occasionally skimming stones, but in a very serious and sad way). Every new moon you would find William in the New Forest, performing a strange dramatic Morris dance with his handkerchiefs that was meant to convey the passage of time and the inherent tragedy of existence (to Arthur it just looked a bit, well, daft, but he was far too polite to tell Woeful William that). And all the days in between? Ten years ago Woeful William had discovered something that had completely and utterly changed his life.

William had discovered video rental shops.

Every night when William wasn't writing poetry, pondering the meaning of life, or dancing with his handkerchiefs, he could be found in the weepy aisle of Max's Movies right in the center of town. The plan was very simple. William would wait for someone to come in and rent the latest tear-jerking movie, and then he would follow the poor person home and settle down for a free night of a sad movie and plentiful tears. Being invisible did have its advantages. Woeful William and his unsuspecting human would set themselves down in front of the telly together, sobbing the whole way through the film. On one occasion William followed the wrong family home by mistake and had ended up not with a sad film about an orphan raised by foxes but instead with the latest James Carefree comedy. The poor family sat down together with their popcorn and fizzy drinks and cried the whole way through the hysterically funny slapstick comedy, never understanding why (William had felt a bit guilty, but by the time he'd realized his mistake he didn't want to leave and miss the end of the film).

Tonight though, being full-moon night, was poetry night, and William sat underneath his tree, paper and quill in hand (William had never liked pens; he thought they took all the drama and romance out of writing, so he still used an enormous ghostly feather to write with).

Arthur crept up behind William's tree unnoticed. William changed his costume to suit his moods (which veered from sad, to miserable, to depressed and back again). Tonight he was wearing a suitably dramatic velvet shirt with impossibly frilly sleeves and was muttering to himself, flapping his handkerchief about as he recited his poem: "Her eyes were full of tears, much like a pub is full of beers ... No, no, that won't do, that's awful. . . . Tears filled up her eyes, like a water balloon in disguise ... No, no, no, useless. Eyes ... Eyes ... Pies? No, no. Flies? Useless! *Useless!*" He cried, crumpling up the piece of paper and throwing it into the air, where it promptly disappeared. He then reached forward and grabbed another sheet, which appeared mysteriously in his hand out of nowhere, and began writing again.

"Are you all right, William?" asked Arthur, and Woeful William looked up, startled. Seeing it was Arthur, he gestured for him to sit down next to him. Arthur cleared a space in the leaves and perched on the roots of the old chestnut tree.

"Grey Arthur! What a marvelous surprise! I'm fine, I'm fine, I'm just trying to conjure up a poem and it's all going frightfully awry. I watched that film with the sinking ship again last night—fantastic movie, so delightfully tragic—and I feel all inspired, but none of the words are falling into place." William made a point of watching the sinking ship film at least once a month, on account of it being deliciously sad. When it had been playing in the cinema he had been completely in his element. Taking full advantage of being invisible, ghosts can (and do!) sneak in to see any film they like for free, and there's nothing a Sadness Summoner enjoys (in a sad way, naturally) more than being surrounded by hundreds of people sobbing. It was sheer miserable delight. "Can you think of a word that rhymes with eyes?" he asked Arthur.

Arthur pondered for a while. "Rice?" he volunteered helpfully. William flashed him a look that said, "Thank You for Trying, but That's Simply Appalling," and Arthur couldn't help but laugh. "You know I'm not very good at poetry."

"Well, I appreciate your effort anyway." Suddenly

William's eyes lit up, and he turned to face Grey Arthur. "I say, what are you doing tomorrow? *My Mother Sold Me to the Circus* is being released in Max's Movies tomorrow. It's an American film all about an awfully sad girl who is sold to the circus by her mother so her mother can buy some more shoes, and this poor girl has to sleep in the same cage as the lions and eat nothing but cardboard for years until she's rescued, but then she dies soon after from a rare lion disease she caught while living in the circus! It's supposed to be the saddest film this year! What do you say, Arthur?"

Arthur, if he was honest, much preferred James Carefree films. "I can't, I'm afraid, William. That's sort of why I've come here to see you—I've got some news!" Arthur grinned at Woeful William. "I've finally worked out what I am!"

"You have? Well, that's fabulous news, Arthur!" He studied Arthur thoughtfully, looking for clues. "You haven't become a Banshee, have you? I never liked Banshees. It's terribly uncouth, shouting all the time."

"No, William, I'm not a Banshee." Arthur sat up straight, grinning proudly. "I am an Invisible Friend!"

William looked at Arthur quizzically, his floppy hair falling into his eyes. "Are you sure?" he asked.

"Of course I am," replied Arthur.

"I've never heard of a ghost being an Invisible

Friend before. You're *definitely* an Invisible Friend?"

"Definitely," said Arthur. "I've even got my very own human boy and everything!"

Woeful William leaned back against the tree and listened carefully as Arthur talked enthusiastically about a human boy with tufty hair called Tom Golden, a bed beneath a bed, lockers and lunchboxes and lectures on history, and all sorts of varied weird events that had happened to him in the past day. Arthur looked so exceptionally happy that for once William tucked his sad thoughts away, out of sight of his grinning friend.

"So there you go," concluded Arthur. "I'm an Invisible Friend! Isn't it exciting?"

William nodded, unsure.

"I knew you'd be pleased for me! So maybe I'll grab a film with you another time, William. I've got to head back now. It's all very busy and time-consuming, this job. I've got an early start with school tomorrow morning, so it won't do staying up all night. I'll come and visit you when I can, let you know how it's going." Arthur got to his feet and waved cheerily at Woeful William. "I'll see you soon!"

"Farewell, young Arthur," said William solemnly, waving his handkerchief with a flourish.

As Arthur's little legs carried him off into the distance, back to his human's house and his secret bed beneath a bed and an early night (which was positively *unheard of* for a ghost), William started work on a new poem.

It was entitled, *"My Friend Has Made Friends with a Human (and It's All Going to End in Tears)."*

A Sock and a Realization

A WEEK PASSED. AT NIGHTTIME GREY ARTHUR WOULD tell Tom stories that he couldn't hear, and when the Cold Fish CD was played Grey Arthur would do a silly dance that Tom couldn't see. Each morning Arthur would quietly accompany Tom on the walk to school. Each isolated lunchtime Arthur would sit by Tom's side and keep the creeping loneliness at bay. If ever Big Ben tried to intimidate or threaten Tom, Arthur found ways to get the nearest teacher's attention. If Tom ever forgot his homework, Arthur would make sure it found its way into his schoolbag before he left the door. If Tom couldn't find something, Arthur would help look too. Grey Arthur peeled many stickers off Tom's back, threw away many notes, and was there at Tom's side every time any of the kids at school called Tom names or shouted abuse. Even though Tom thought he was very much alone, he wasn't.

Grey Arthur was a very good friend indeed, apart from the slight problem of Tom not knowing he existed.

Life was pretty good.

So seven days passed from the time they met (which is of course a reasonably long time for a human boy, and a mere blink of the eye for a ghost), which lands us firmly on yet another Tuesday. Grey Arthur was settled by the bed, huddled by the glow of the night-light, telling Tom a story all about the antics of the legendary Red Rascal in a voice that Tom couldn't hear. Tom had already settled down to get to sleep, and this unheard bedtime story was a ritual each night. Tom yawned and snuggled under the covers, and his eyes slowly closed.

"And so the elephant was returned the next day, and none of the humans were any the wiser," concluded Arthur. It was one of his favorite stories, The Red Rascal and the Elephant's Exodus, although it was closely followed by the legendary Red Rascal and the Disappearing Building episode (not such a catchy title, but what's not to love about a Poltergeist who can move a whole office block). Content that Tom was fast asleep, Arthur was just about to crawl into his bed beneath the bed when he heard something. There was a rustling coming from the laundry basket in the corner of the room. Suddenly the lid of the basket flew up into the air, and out crawled Miranda and Mike, dragging out all the dirty clothes with them. The Mischief Twins had arrived.

The Mischief Twins were Poltergeists-in-training, and the Laundry Run was something all Poltergeists have to do when they first start out. It's a well-known ghost fact (and a very little-known human one) that all laundry baskets are magically connected together, and Poltergeists can "ride" laundry baskets to pop from house to house, which is very handy for the harvesting of socks. Many different ghosts have many different portals like this, from mushroom rings, to the ends of rainbows, magic mirrors, lucky stones, wishing wells, each one a door, a connection to somewhere else—and Grey Arthur hadn't mastered the art of using a single one of them. Poor Grey Arthur had to run everywhere. Still, he got to see the sights and he liked the fresh air, so he never complained. He'd never even attempted Laundry Traveling during the time he'd tried to be a Poltergeist, because the thought of traveling through Grandma's stockings and Dad's sweaty work clothes to get from house to house seemed fairly disgusting to him. Poltergeists tended to do it all the time, though. It was their trademark.

And so it was that this very night Laundry Traveling had taken these two particular young

Poltergeists straight into the bedroom of Tom Golden at 11 Aubergine Road.

Miranda and Mike, the Mischief Twins, were dressed from head to toe in outfits made entirely from odd socks stitched together. Miranda's bright orange hair was tied up in pigtails using different-colored soccer socks, and Mike's mop of blue hair was emphasized by a green rugby sock tied around his head. They looked like normal children, if slightly pinker than usual, twice as dirty, and three times as mischievous. They tumbled to the floor, giggling, spilling clothes all around them, and immediately set to work (Poltergeists might visit up to fifteen houses a night, so they didn't have time to waste). Mike was deciding which socks they were going to steal and which to leave behind, and Miranda was trying on one of Tom's favorite T-shirts, while hiding a red sock inside a white school shirt. They were so busy giggling that they didn't notice Grey Arthur. But then not many people did.

Not until he shouted.

"Put them back!" he yelled. Miranda and Mike froze, and turned to face him. Seeing who it was, Mike grinned. Miranda had just been about to smudge a stain on Tom's favorite T-shirt—something dark and sticky that most definitely wouldn't come out in the wash. Seeing Arthur, she smiled sweetly and put the dark sticky mess back in her pocket.

"Grey Arthur! Good to see you! Well, most of you. Is it me, or are you getting less see-through?" asked Miranda, not waiting for an answer before carrying on. "What are you doing here, anyway? I thought you gave up trying to be a Poltergeist. If you're after his socks, you'll have to join the queue."

Miranda sniffed a sock tentatively, then laughed as she threw it in Mike's face. Mike grabbed it and flicked Miranda around the ear with it, and they both collapsed in fits of giggles.

"Put them back! Put Tom's clothes back right now!" yelled Arthur, trying to snatch the socks back from them. Tom stirred in his sleep but didn't wake, unable to hear any of the argument being waged over his dirty laundry.

"What? Why do you care, Arthur?" asked Mike. "We're just collecting a few socks. That's what we do. He's just a human, he won't miss them."

"He's my friend," shouted Arthur, as Miranda and Mike began filling their pockets with odd socks. "You can't steal his socks! Put his socks back right now!"

Mike and Miranda both stopped and looked at Grey Arthur, who was so annoyed by now that he was beginning to turn from grey to fizzing red.

"What?" asked Miranda, her forehead all creased with confusion. "How is he your friend, Arthur?"

"He doesn't even know you exist," said Mike dismissively.

"I'm his Invisible Friend, if you must know!" retorted Grey Arthur, and for a moment Miranda and Mike said nothing.

Just for a moment.

Then they burst out laughing so loudly that, if Tom had been able to hear them, he most definitely would have woken up. Mike laughed so hard that he forgot he was sitting on the floor, and he floated up in the air and rolled across the ceiling, holding his sides. Miranda laughed until tears streamed down her face, leaving clean traces in all the dirt.

"What?" demanded Arthur. "What is it? Why are you laughing at me?"

"You don't get it, doofus!" gasped Miranda, in between fits of giggles. Mike laughed so hard he bashed into the light in the ceiling, and even then he couldn't stop giggling. Grey Arthur turned a darker shade of red.

"What?!" demanded Arthur. "What is it? Tell me!"

Miranda took a deep breath, trying to suppress her laughter. She put on the expression that Arthur recognized as the one that Mrs. Lemon used in school when she had to explain something very simple to someone for the tenth time. "Human children," said Miranda slowly, trying to keep the grin from her face, "have invisible friends that *only they can see*." She paused to let this sink in. "They Are Imaginary. That's why they're called invisible! They don't *really* exist!"

Arthur stared back at her, confused, shaking his head. His red began to fade. "You've got it wrong, Miranda," he said, although horrible doubt was beginning to crawl in around the edges. Surely they'd got it wrong? They had to.

"You, Arthur, are a ghost." Mike chuckled, slowly floating down from the ceiling to face Arthur. "Humans can't see ghosts. He can't see you, he can't hear you, he doesn't know you're there. It doesn't make you his Invisible Friend, Arthur, just because you're invisible. *You can't be his friend if he doesn't even know that you're there!*"

Those words finally struck home, and they carried with them more than a fair share of sadness. Arthur's bottom lip began to quiver. How could he have got it so wrong? His red color had entirely disappeared now, and he began to take on a hint of blue. He sat down cross-legged on the floor. Miranda and Mike's giggling faded in the air, leaving only an awkward silence. Mischief is one thing, giggles another, but misery, and deep sighs, and sadness are another thing altogether, and not something Poltergeists like at all. Realizing how miserable they had made Arthur, the twins began to feel more than a little bit guilty. Seeing Grey Arthur all blue took the laughter out of them.

"I'm sorry, Arthur, we shouldn't have made fun of you like that," apologized Mike.

"We didn't intend to be mean, it's just, well, you got it so muddled," said Miranda. Arthur stared at the floor, getting bluer by the second. They were right, though. His supposed best friend didn't even know who he was. He'd been so stupid, so very stupid: a poor excuse for a ghost and a poor excuse for an Invisible Friend. He'd been so excited to find something he could be, something he could do, that he forgot to think about all the other things that were important. He wanted to just sink through the floor and keep on falling forever. Mike and Miranda looked awkwardly at the ground.

"Well, erm, we've got to be off now, Arthur," said Mike. Arthur nodded feebly, not looking up. "Do you mind if we take a few socks?"

"Sure," said Arthur miserably. "What does it matter?"

Miranda and Mike took what they wanted and carefully put all the rest of the clothes back into the laundry basket. Nobody would know they had ever been there, they were so careful to leave everything as they'd found it, minus the stolen socks. Mike took Tom's front door keys and hid them underneath his shoes. Miranda left a glass of water that had been by Tom's night table right on the edge of his desk, balanced precariously. Satisfied that their Poltergeisting duties were done, they stood back to admire their work and nodded to each other. Miranda and Mike were currently at the top of their class in Poltergeist training, and there was no doubt why. The Mischief Twins had struck again.

Just before they left, Miranda came up to Arthur and pressed something into his hand.

"To cheer you up," she said. In Arthur's hand was a white sock with gold stitching and a little emblem sewn on the ankle. He looked up, confused.

"She got it last week," said Mike. "We went on a trip to the palace. Hugest laundry baskets you've ever seen! That there is a royal sock, Arthur."

"A lucky sock. To say sorry, for being mean," said Miranda. With a grin, she jumped into the laundry basket and was gone. Mike waved and jumped in after her.

Arthur studied the sock. He sniffed it, expecting it to smell of gold, and royalty, and flowers. It smelled of foot. *Royal* foot. He turned a little less blue but still felt down in the dumps. He put the sock in his pocket and crawled under Tom's bed to go to sleep. Tomorrow he would think about whether or not they were really friends. Tomorrow he would decide what he should do. Tonight he just felt like curling up in a ball underneath Tom's bed, with the old comics and the soft toys that Tom insisted he was far too old for now (but that Mum wasn't allowed to throw away). Grey Arthur snuggled underneath the bed, tinged blue and feeling sorry for himself, and he felt like maybe he could have been a Sadness Summoner after all.

A Bad Luck Day

WEDNESDAY STARTED TERRIBLY FOR TOM. WELL, TO
be honest, it started pretty much the same as every
other school day before it. The alarm beeped to life,
and Tom groggily reached out and turned it to
snooze. Five minutes later the alarm went off again,
and Tom reached out and turned it off again.

"Come on, lazybones, out of bed." Tom's mum
strode into the room and pulled open the curtains, letting light stream into the room. Tom winced and
rolled over, pretending to be still asleep. "No, you
don't. Come on, out of bed." This routine was played
out, pretty much word for word, every single morning, and so this wasn't the point where the day started
to go wrong. No, that happened when Tom's mum left
the room just a fraction too soon, just before Tom had
gotten all the way out of bed, and so as soon as the
door shut Tom settled down and went back to sleep.
He finally got woken up again when his pillow fell off
the bed from underneath his head (which was very
strange indeed, but Tom was a bit too sleepy to appreciate just how odd that was). Blearily, Tom peered at
his alarm clock.

8:10 . . .

8:10!

Tom was going to be late. His heart jolted with

fear, and he quickly jumped out of bed. This was the stage at which things started going wrong properly. He got washed and dived into his uniform, and had only just buttoned up his sleeves when he managed to brush against a glass on the edge of his desk and spill water all over himself. He hadn't remembered leaving the glass there, but it was too late now—he was soaked to the skin. Mother tutted, and managed to find him another shirt to wear, but the only one she could find was slightly too small, and the buttons gaped at the chest and the sleeves refused to do up.

"It's too late now, Tom, you'll have to make do," Mum said as she gave up on trying to do up his shirt-sleeves. Tom sighed deeply and bounded back up the stairs to pack his bag. The next thing that happened was that he couldn't find his keys, no matter how hard he looked. In the end he gave up, precious time wasted, and went to grab a pair of socks.

"Argh," he muttered to himself as he rummaged through his drawer. "Why is it you can never find a pair of socks when you need to?" In his hand he clutched one odd white sock, which was the color they had to wear with their uniform, and yet all the other socks in the drawer seemed to be blue or green or black. He had just about given up when something caught his attention.

Laid out on his bed was a single white sock.

He could have sworn it hadn't been there a second

ago. It was pretty much plain white, except for a little gold emblem and some letters stitched on it (HRH? What on earth does that stand for?). Tom decided it would have to do. He slipped on the socks, and when he went to put on his shoes he found his keys underneath them.

"How weird is that?" said Tom to himself. He glanced at the alarm clock: 8:20.

Tom was late. He sprinted down the stairs, shouted a good-bye to Mum and Dad, and rushed out the door.

In the hallway, forgotten, sat his packed lunch. It was going to be one of those days.

School was no better. Nobody would let him forget the time he called Mr. Hammond "Dad," even though it had been nearly a week ago. As Tom rushed into school toward his locker, he saw people gathered around it, giggling. Tom sighed. The kids saw him approaching and quickly dispersed, snorting with barely contained laughter, and Tom walked up to his locker, trying to catch his breath. Someone had stuck a poster on his locker that read I LOVE DAD! in big red letters, with little hearts drawn all around it. Tom scrunched it up and threw it away, but as he walked through the corridor he still heard people giggling about it. His cheeks burned red. At that exact moment a button popped off his shirt, pinging across the corridor, and Tom just winced, wishing he could have stayed in bed. . . .

The lessons rolled on, and soon it was lunchtime. This was when Tom realized he had forgotten his packed lunch, and he had only fifteen pence on him, since the rest of his money had fallen through a hole in his trouser pocket. Becky Chance, a very pretty girl from class F, offered him some of her lunch, but only if he "barked like a dog." The other kids laughed at that and waited expectantly. Tom refused, and instead sat alone under a tree in the playground, just him and his growling stomach. Mum and Dad were both at work, so there was nothing more for him to do. Lunchtimes go really slowly when you have nothing to eat and nobody to talk to.

Then he got the results back from his history test in fifth lesson, from Mr. Hammond. He'd gotten a D. The teacher offered to talk him through the results, but Tom made some excuse about having to be somewhere else very urgently—if the other kids saw him talking to "Dad" alone, he'd never hear the end of it. He left as quickly as possible, stomach growling, tight shirt with a button missing clinging to his chest, in his hand clutching a failed test, and realized as well that he'd somehow managed to lose all his pen caps somewhere in that classroom, and all his pens had leaked inside his pencil case. What a wretched day. . . . Not long now until today was over, though.

The final lesson was music, which is usually good fun, but today the teacher was off sick, and the substitute teacher was a woman with weirdly hairy arms, who talked so slowly that you felt like you were being forced to sleep. Tom's eyes rolled in his head as he struggled to stay awake.

Must . . . pay . . . attention . . .

. . .

. . . . . .

. . . .

Tom didn't realize he had fallen asleep. Well, not until he woke up. He felt his table shudder, as if someone had nudged it—which was impossible because he was sitting by himself—and he realized he was dribbling on his notebook.

"Am I boring you, Tom?" asked the strangely hairy teacher, and Tom sat up so fast that another two buttons popped off his shirt. They bounced off the desk in front of him, and one even managed to hit Jenny Smith on the back of the head. His shirt now practically fell open at the chest. The class burst into hysterical laughter at that point. Tom just gritted his teeth and stared at the desk, blushing. The laughter didn't disappear; in fact, the redder he got, the more they laughed, and although the hairy teacher tried to regain control (*"Quiet, class. I said quiet. Stop laughing. Right, that's it. Detention for the next person who laughs. Why are you ignoring me?" she droned in her dull voice*) it was impossible to break the hysteria that had gripped the class at Tom's expense. Wheezy Thomson even had to go see the school nurse, as he laughed so much he had a mild asthma attack, but even as he sucked on his inhaler in the sick bay, the tears that streamed down his face were from laughing and not from being ill.

The last lesson seemed to drag on forever. When the laughter had finally died down (and even then it would sometimes erupt in pockets throughout the classroom, usually started by someone saying *"Ping!"* and miming a button flying through the air, or by simply looking at the tattered shirt that was now held together by three but-tons and a safety pin lent by Strangely Hairy Teacher), Tom couldn't wait to be going home.

When the final bell rang to signal the end of school, Tom felt that it had been One of the Worst Days Ever, and that it couldn't possibly get any worse.

How wrong he was.

The Spitting Kids were waiting on the corner as he walked home from school. The Spitting Kids were pretty much a local feature, although you could never predict exactly where you would find them—gathered on a street corner, outside a shop, at the local park, at the bus shelter, or by a particular street lamp. Bad luck had just thrown them in Tom's path today. As ever, all dressed in white, baseball caps all pulled down over their eyes, they were swearing and spitting and shout-ing at people who tried to get past. Tom's heart sank, and he looked down at the ground, desperate to avoid their attention. Everyone knew who the Spitting Kids were, even Tom, who had lived there for only a few weeks, and everyone knew to avoid them in the same way you avoid angry dogs, licking metal poles on winter days, and playing on train tracks.

Only today it was much worse. Today one of the Spitting Kids was Big Ben.

Big Ben stood tall above the others, smoking and spitting in equal turns, a recognizable glare from among a crowd of fierce faces. The precise people who made up the Spitting Kids were in constant flux, new faces joining one day and sometimes leaving the next; a nameless mass all wearing baseball caps and angry scowls, a choir of spitting and swearing and aggression. Sometimes one of the older ones would have a moped, and they would rev the engine and speed up and down the road. Sometimes they would drink from cans and flick cigarette butts at people who walked past. Today they were mostly spitting, the pavement glistening foully, and shouting insults at those unfortunate enough to catch their attention. And there, at the center of them, was Big Ben, sucking deeply on a cigarette. Fear rattled inside Tom's chest. *Head down, head down, keep on walking, Tom. They might not see you,* he thought to himself.

"Oi, Freak Boy! Nice shirt, Freak Boy!" yelled one of the Spitting Kids, and as the others saw Tom and his ragged shirt they howled with laughter. Tom's heart lurched. No chance of not being spotted now. The

Spitting Kids walked out to block off the pavement, and there was no way past them. Panic surged within Tom, and his mouth dried. One of them tugged on Tom's sleeve, and another button fell free, prompting even more laughter. The laughter didn't hold any humor or joy in it, though. The laughter sounded like hyenas. "This the one you was talking about, Ben?" Tom glanced up nervously to see Big Ben pushing his way through the group.

"That's the one. Black eye I gave him's almost gone now. Do you reckon I should give him a new one?"

More laughter. Tom's lungs felt tight, like he couldn't get enough air.

"What d'you reckon, Freak Boy? Want another black eye? Or do you wanna give us some money instead? Your call."

Big Ben had been the first person to ever call him a freak, and this name had spread and spread through-out the school and now outside the school, until almost everybody called Tom "Freak Boy" now. People he'd never even met before called him a freak. Bullying is contagious in that way sometimes, like hair lice or warts. Each time Tom heard that name, he winced. *Freak Boy.* At night it would rattle around in his head, rolling over and over. *Freak Boy* . . . Big Ben was holding his hand out expectantly, snapping his fingers, with that horrid hyena laughter rattling in the background. He grinned nastily, stained teeth, stale smoke breath. Tom still had the fifteen pence left in his pocket, and part of him wanted to just hand it over and get away, get home, close his bedroom door and shut himself away, but today had been such an awful day, such a wretched day, a day of misery, and upset, and loneliness, and harsh laughter, that something inside Tom broke.

"You're not big, you're not clever, and you're not impressing ANYONE, Ben!" screamed Tom. The sound of his own voice surprised him. Tom hadn't meant to say anything, hadn't realized he was saying anything until he heard the angry words in his own voice. It was something Mum had always said when Tom misbehaved, and here he was throwing it back at the Spitting Kids. As soon as the words were free he regretted them, but you can't take back these things. What is said is said.

The Spitting Kids gasped in mock horror, and Tom began to desperately wish he hadn't said a thing. Big Ben simply locked those dark, angry eyes on Tom, his lips curling back from his yellowing teeth like a dog about to bite. The way home was blocked off, and he couldn't get past the Spitting Kids, couldn't get past Big Ben. That was when everything *really* took a turn for the worse. Big Ben leaned down, his eyes locked with Tom's, and picked up a broken bottle off the ground. Tom's heart began to pound frantically, and his legs started to feel wobbly. Tears pricked at his eyes, and cold fear gathered in the pit of his stomach.

Grey Arthur, who had followed Tom around all day in a sad mood, trying to work out if they were really friends or not, whether he was a good Invisible Friend or not, stood next to Tom, not that Tom knew it. Grey Arthur was screaming at Tom, not that Tom could hear it, screaming so hard that he felt the words were pounding themselves into the air.

"RUN!" screamed Grey Arthur. "Run, Tom! RUN!" Tom was frozen, feet stuck heavily to the ground with terror, and even if he could have heard Grey Arthur shouting in his ear, chances are he wouldn't have been able to do anything anyway. His heart hammered in his chest, his tongue clung dryly to the inside of his mouth, and his legs were heavier than concrete.

"What did you say to me?" spat Big Ben, his face centimeters away from Tom's. He stank of overflowing ashtray. Tom winced. The bottle waved perilously close to Tom's face, so close he could smell the drink it used to hold. "You wanna start something, do you? Freak Boy. Do you?" He brought the smashed bottle up even closer, and Tom felt tears begin to roll down his cheeks. Some of the Spitting Kids laughed. Some encouraged Big Ben on. Some simply watched, all vicious grins and wide eyes.

Grey Arthur was screaming and screaming, but nobody could hear him. He felt utterly helpless.

There were no teachers nearby. No time to get help. Nothing he could do. Ghosts can't touch humans. That was ghost fact. There was nothing around, nothing he could throw, nothing at all. "Think, Grey Arthur," he told himself urgently. *"THINK!"*

And then it came to him, in a flash.

Ghosts can't touch humans, that was ghost fact, but ghosts *can* touch clothes. The Mischief Twins spent their lives touching clothes. Grey Arthur ran behind Big Ben and grabbed hold of the hood to his top. Using every inch of his ghostly strength he pulled as hard as he possibly could. Usually Grey Arthur wasn't renowned for his strength, but he was so worried for his friend, so angry, so concerned, that when he pulled on that hood as hard as he possibly could Big Ben was lifted off his feet and yanked backward through the air. The bottle tumbled free from his hand and smashed harmlessly to the ground.

The Spitting Kids looked on, astounded to see Big Ben flying through the air, his huge arms flailing, for no apparent reason.

Tom was just as amazed, but he had no time to stand and watch Big Ben colliding with the ground. The distraction had given him just the moment he'd been waiting for. He lifted his heavy legs, and he ran.

He ran and ran, faster than the time he ran the hundred meters, faster than he'd ever run before, feet slamming into the ground, faster, faster. Behind him he could hear the Spitting Kids shouting and giving chase, but he ran on, the wind whistling in his ears, everything blurring because of the speed at which he was hurtling through the streets back to home. Past the phone box, past the abandoned house on the corner, onward, faster, *faster*. He ran like an Olympic athlete, like a tiger chasing through the forest, like a scared boy running from his bullies, and to this very day Tom will tell you, if you ask him, that he ran faster than anyone had ever run before in the history of mankind. He probably would have made it home in record-breaking time too.

Had the car not hit him.

Tom, racing across a road, was so determined to get home and safe that he forgot that cars go on roads and humans go on pavements, and he ran flat out into the road without looking. Time slowed to a virtual halt then, and the few things Tom remembers are as follows: seeing the car out of the corner of his eye, putting his hands out in front of him, and then lying in the road while the woman who had been driving the car was trying to make sure he was all right. He felt very distant, slightly faded, and not very awake, and he was sure he saw the strangest-looking boy with lopsided ears and misshapen hair standing over him, looking very concerned and more than a little see-through. Tom tried to smile at him, to let him know that he was okay, but he felt so strange and woozy that he didn't quite manage it. His lips felt numb.

Everything faded to black.

Hospital

GREY ARTHUR WAITED AGITATEDLY AT THE HOSPITAL. Tom had been taken there in a big noisy vehicle with flashing lights and given a bed in a ward very quickly, but he still hadn't woken up properly. The doctors had shone lights, and done tests, and examined him from head to toe, but now everything just had to be left to waiting. Time trickled slowly on. Tom looked quite pale, and smaller than usual, and although he was tucked up underneath a blanket he still looked cold. Arthur had heard the doctor telling his parents that until Tom woke up they couldn't really be sure how broken he was. Tom's parents looked very upset, and both had the same red, puffy eyes that Tom had had the night Arthur met him. Tom's dad paced up and down anxiously, while Tom's mum locked her hands around her handbag, knuckles turning white, and stood still like a statue, waiting for Tom to wake up.

They weren't the only ones waiting. At the end of Tom's bed Grey Arthur had taken up his vigil, and everything inside him felt all in knots. Ghosts don't get ill or hurt like humans do, so all these horrible fears were new to Arthur, and he was beside himself with worry for his little human friend. It was the worst feeling in the world. Woeful William had volunteered to come and keep Arthur company while he waited, but while Arthur had been grateful for the offer, he had said it was better if William didn't come. Tom's parents were sad enough as it was without having to share a room with a Sadness Summoner. William understood, and so instead he waited outside the hospital, reciting his poetry to the begonias and the pigeons.

Eventually Tom's parents became so tired they couldn't stay awake any longer no matter how hard they struggled against it, and they fell asleep on uncomfortable-looking plastic chairs out in the hallway. Grey Arthur stood alone by Tom's bed, willing him to wake up. Hours passed, which to humans is a long time, and which to ghosts isn't very long at all. To Grey Arthur it felt like the longest stretch of time he had ever been through.

Just when sunlight was beginning to creep around the outskirts of the night and the sun was about to drag itself up the sky, Tom began to wake up. Slowly at first, his eyes began to flicker, then gradually he began to open them, blinking away the beginnings of morning light. Everything looked foggy at first, like opening your eyes underwater, and even when the fog began to clear Tom didn't recognize where he was. There were curtains all around him, and he was lying in a bed that didn't feel like his own. The memory of the car crash suddenly fell into place with a jolt, and Tom realized where he must be.

Hospital.

The funny-faced boy with the uneven ears and strange hair was here again. He looked a little blurry and a little lacking in color, but Tom thought that might be because he had taken quite a bang on the head. Maybe it would take a while for his eyes to get back to normal.

"Hello," croaked Tom, his voice shaky.

Grey Arthur nearly jumped a mile. Tom was staring *straight at him*! Surely this wasn't possible? Surely this was impossible! Arthur looked around, but there was nobody else there apart from him, so he couldn't be looking at anyone else. Tom could see him! *Tom could see him!* Arthur brushed out the creases in his ghostly outfit, smoothed down his ghostly hair, and concentrated as hard as possible to look as normal as possible. He smiled nervously back at Tom.

"You can see me?" he asked, and Tom tried to nod, but moving his head hurt so much that it was nearly impossible.

"I'm not blind," Tom said, his voice little more

than a whisper. "Who are you? I saw you earlier, I'm sure, just after the crash . . ."

Grey Arthur stood up as tall as he could and grinned from ear to ear (a little too literally, perhaps, but Tom was still groggy and didn't appear to notice).

"I," said Arthur, with the biggest smile in the world, "am your Invisible Friend!"

Tom smiled back, a little nervously, and wondered just how hard he had hit his head.

Everything Will Make More Sense in the Morning

TOM WASN'T SURE WHERE BEING AWAKE ENDED AND being asleep began. Broken bottles, car crashes, a strange boy with a wide smile and all in muted grey . . . Tom's sleep was dark and strange and full of weird dreams and vague shapes.

His sleep felt heavy and sticky, like molasses, and it was hard to wake up, hard to escape from. Each time he thought he was nearly awake, something else happened to convince him he was still dreaming. Lights being shined in his eyes . . . Feelings of spinning, or falling, or floating . . . Once he swore he saw a nurse walk past with a laundry trolley, from out of which crawled two children in the oddest outfits, giggling, who fled clutching some clothes. The nurse had walked on, oblivious, humming to herself . . . People asking him the date, the year, his name . . . Strange dreams, all dark around the edges . . .

Finally, though, he felt his eyes flicker, and the dreams were chased away. . . .

"He's waking up. . . . He's waking up."

"Well, don't crowd him then, give him some space."

"I'm not crowding him. Tom, can you hear us, honey? Tom, it's Mummy."

"And Daddy. We're both here. How's your head, son?"

"Don't ask him questions yet, let him wake up first. How are you feeling, Tom?"

"I thought you said not to ask him questions."

"It's not really a question, is it? It's more a statement of concern. It's just something mothers say. I just want to make sure he's okay."

"Stop flapping, he's fine. Aren't you, Tom? How are you feeling, Tom?"

"Don't crowd him, give him some space."

"That's what I said to you!"

Tom woke up to find his mum and dad peering at him with worried looks only just kept at bay by tired smiles. Mum was holding a bunch of grapes, enough sports drink to rehydrate a desert, and a rather sorry-looking potted plant (she'd explain later that it was the last one in the shop, though why she thought Tom wanted a potted plant was never actually touched on). Mum was bubbling with nervous energy and desperately looked like she wanted to spit on a tissue and clean Tom to within an inch of his life. Dad, on the other hand, looked weary, and the beginning of a beard made him look older. He was clutching an empty Styrofoam cup that once had been home to some of the world's most potent/repulsive coffee, and tucked under his other arm seemed to be every single newspaper in the entire hospital. Tom tried to smile to show his parents that he was okay, but the smile was thin and fleeting. His head was pounding.

"Hey, Mum. Hey, Dad," he said, in his best attempt at a strong, healthy voice. It was meant to sound reassuring, but it didn't. It sounded weak and wobbly. His mouth was awfully dry. Mum's eyes filled with tears as Tom spoke, although she blinked them away as best as possible. Tom had never seen his parents like this before. He was used to them smiling, or laughing, or occasionally shouting, but never before had he seen these dark, tired eyes, seen their faces look so dusted with shadows or heavy with worry.

"You gave us such a fright, Tom!" Mum said, her

voice wavering. Dad put his arm around her and squeezed gently.

"I'm so sorry," Tom whispered.

"No, no, don't be daft," said Dad quickly. "Nothing to be sorry about. We're just glad you're okay. The doctor will be round to see you in a bit, just to do a few more tests, just to be sure. You took quite a knock."

"My head hurts. And my hands," mumbled Tom.

"They would do, sweetheart," said Mum, gently touching Tom's cheek. "But the doctor said that you haven't actually broken anything. She was very surprised at that. She said you'd been incredibly lucky."

Tom didn't feel lucky. Tom felt like he'd been hit by a car.

"Do you want to tell us what happened?" asked Dad, settling himself down on the edge of the bed.

"I ... um ..." Tom hesitated. Mum and Dad looked at him encouragingly, quietly nodding as they waited for him to speak. "I didn't look where I was going. I must have been daydreaming or something. I just ran in front of a car. Stupid, really. I'm sorry."

"No point apologizing about it. You're fine, and that's the main thing," said Mum gently. Everything began to catch up with Tom then, the worry, the pain, and his bottom lip began to wobble. Tears started to form. "Hey, hey, don't cry, Tom. I know, you've had a rough old day, but I've got something here to cheer you up. Your teacher popped in earlier on, uh, oh, what's his name . . ."

"The beardy one," interrupted Dad. Mum subtly nudged him in the ribs with her elbow. Apparently you shouldn't refer to teachers as "beardy ones."

"Oh, Mr. Hammond." Tom sniffed.

"That's it, Mr. Hammond," Mum agreed. "He came in and brought a Get Well card for you. Seems he got the whole class to sign it too."

Mum rummaged in her handbag and finally pulled out a large card in a bright yellow envelope. TOM GOLDEN it read, in big, neat letters on the front. Although his hands were sore and bruised, Tom still managed to grin as he tore open the envelope and retrieved the card inside.

On the front there was a picture of an elephant with a bandaged head, sitting in a hospital bed. All around him were different animal friends, clutching balloons, or flowers, or chocolates, all wearing big smiles. In massive, bright letters at the top of the card it shouted GET WELL SOON! Tom smiled at his parents. Maybe some good had come from this crash? Maybe now people would realize how mean they had been? Maybe people would actually want to be his friends now? Tom looked at the picture of the smiling animal friends all gathered around the bed and gently opened the card.

Inside, it simply read:

Tom,
Get well soon.
From Mr. Hammond and Class B.

Beneath, all the children in the class had simply, uniformly signed their names. Sarah. John. Kate. Adam . . . No personal messages, no little illustrations, no "Hope you're feeling better!" or even a "We'll miss you!" Peter. Alex. Toby. Marianne . . . Just name after name. Not a friend in sight.

"See, isn't that nice of them, Tom?" Mum said with a smile. Parents can be daft like that sometimes, and Tom didn't have the heart to tell her that the card wasn't nice at all. As he closed the card, though, he noticed something on the back. A trail of inky smudged fingerprints decorated the card, and nestled in among them was a small message. The writing was terrible—it looked like someone had submerged a spider in a puddle of ink and then chased it across the page, but if Tom held the card up close and squinted he could just about make out what it said:

Tom i hope you are feeling
beTTer soon and ThaT The car
didnT hurT To much and ThaT
you will be bak in class soon.

love BallpoinT Bill

Tom had never even heard of Ballpoint Bill before. "Is there a new boy in class?"

"I don't think so, Tom," said Dad, taking the card and placing it on the bedside cabinet. It stood next to the potted plant, which was busy dropping leaves already and looking forlorn. "Anyway, you should get some rest."

"Yes," added Mum. "You don't want to overdo it. Try and get some more sleep before the doctor comes round, eh?"

"Okay, I'll try," promised Tom. "Oh, by the way, Mum, Dad—there was a boy here earlier. A really strange-looking boy. Did you see where he went?"

Mum and Dad shared confused looks.

"I didn't see any boy here, Tom. You sure you didn't dream it?"

"I don't know. Possibly. Probably," conceded Tom. It *had* been an odd night's sleep. "I must have just got confused."

"Not surprising really, after what you've been through." Mum knelt over and ever so gently kissed Tom on the forehead. "Oh, I know, I know, you're too old for kisses, but just this once. Okay?"

"Okay," agreed Tom. They shared a smile.

"We'll just be in the corridor if you need us," Dad added.

Tom didn't, though. Pretty much as soon as his parents stepped out into the corridor, he was already asleep again. This time he didn't dream of strange boys, or stolen laundry, or cars, or flashing lights. This time he dreamed of tigers carrying balloons, and hippos with flowers, and a giraffe with a box of chocolates as a get-well present for him. And even though Tom knew this dream was just a dream, he liked it all the same.

Hometime

TOM WAS MADE TO STAY IN THE HOSPITAL FOR ONE more night, just so the doctors could keep an eye on him, but other than some bruising they couldn't find anything else the matter with him. Everyone kept on telling Tom just how lucky he had been, but he didn't consider being struck by a car in the first place as good luck at all, so he just nodded quietly and waited to go home. Other than his parents, he'd not had any visitors while he'd been in the hospital—he'd not even seen that strange boy again, so he supposed his parents must have been right. Nothing more than a dream.

The doctors said he'd be able to go back to school the next day.

"Isn't that good news?" his parents had said to Tom excitedly, and Tom had tried his hardest to look enthused, but deep down he'd felt a little pang of terror. As they drove home now, the radio cheerily belting out songs, Tom tried to tuck the worry and sadness he felt out of sight. Mum and Dad made small talk, and Dad would smile at him through the rearview mirror whenever he caught Tom's gaze, but other than that a heavy silence settled on Tom. He didn't want to go back to school. He couldn't face going back there on his own.

It was nice to be home, though. It was nice to be back at that familiar front door, to smell the smell of your house (as everyone knows, every house smells different, and 11 Aubergine Road smelled like home, whereas the hospital smelled of disinfectant, and squeaky floors, and congealing dinners). It was nice to go up those familiar stairs, to the door with the KEEP OUT sign taped to it. It was nice to go through that door and shut it behind him, and be safely tucked away in his own familiar room.

Except something was different. Something wasn't familiar, and old, and trusty. Something—and it took Tom a while to work out what—*something* had changed.

The photos!

On the far wall above Tom's desk was his photo collage. He stuck all the photos he liked up there, pictures of old birthdays and summers spent by the sea, photos of climbing trees and busted knees and just an assortment of memories. Pinned up on the board was a new photo, though, obviously put up there by Mum and Dad to welcome him home. A picture taken last week, of Tom in his new uniform, grinning goofily at the camera. He remembered having that picture taken—he was just rushing out the door, and Dad had called him back into the kitchen and made him stand still until he'd used up the last of his film. Tom's eye still had a hint of purple in the picture, and his tuft of hair was certainly visible, but that wasn't the thing that made him get goose bumps. As he stared silently at the photo, his mouth dropped open.

Tom wasn't alone in the picture.

Behind him, grinning wildly, was a boy. The boy looked like he had leaped from a black-and-white photograph, though, and his hair looked even more ridiculous than Tom's tuft. Something about that boy stirred a memory, and as Tom stared he realized where he recognized him from—he was the boy at the hospital! The boy who had also been at the car crash! But . . . that was impossible. Tom had been alone when that photo was taken. How could the other boy possibly have been there? What was . . .

A rustling from underneath Tom's bed made his train of thought stop dead. His heart began to race, and he held his breath.

What happened next is something Tom will go

over and over in his mind many, many times in the future. Although he'll try very hard to find the right words to explain the momentous outright *weirdness* of it all, there are some events that are so abstract that they flit on the outskirts of being describable.

But if Tom were to describe what happened next, this is probably how he'd do it.

From underneath the bed leaped a boy, *the* boy, the one who had been at the car crash. The one at the hospital. *The one in the photo.* He was all dusty colors and smudges of grey, and now that Tom could see him properly he noted with shock that this boy was slightly see-through. His ears were on wonky, and his hair looked as if each individual strand had decided to grow in a different direction. He was a little bit taller than Tom, although not much, and he was dressed like something from an old book. The strange boy was clutching something as he emerged from beneath the bed, and as Tom finally managed to peel his eyes away from the strangeness of him, he realized he was holding a card.

It had been made from a scrap of paper, some fluff from underneath the bed, and some old sweet wrappers from the wastepaper basket. It was so amateur that Tom suspected that if the boy breathed too heavily it might crumble to pieces, but then the strange boy didn't actually seem to be breathing. WELCOME HOME FROM YOUR BEST FRIEND, read the messy handwriting at the top of the card.

"Surprise!" yelled Grey Arthur.

Tom made a squeaking noise that might have made it into a full-fledged scream if he hadn't been so shocked.

How do you describe the feeling you only get at Christmas? How do you describe what you felt the first time you saw the sea? Or how you felt the first time you got lost from your parents as a child? Some things are simply too *big* to properly cram inside words. How do you explain how you feel when a ghost leaps out from underneath your bed, clutching a welcome home card he's obviously made himself?

Scared. Amazed. Amused. Bemused. Confused. Gravity loosened its grip a little, and Tom's head spun. His mouth dried, and his lips moved silently like a goldfish as he desperately hoped words would come.

None did. Instead he gawked hopelessly at Grey Arthur, whose smile was slowly fading from his face.

"Don't you like the card?"

BOOK TWO

• • • • •

All Change

So Where Do We Go from Here?

FOR WHAT FELT LIKE THE LONGEST TIME, NOTHING happened. The two boys, one ghost, one real, faced each other in silence. Then, without even thinking, Tom reached out to the nearest thing at hand (which was, in this instance, his old cactus plant) and threw it at Grey Arthur. It glided through the air and straight through Arthur, causing him to flicker slightly, like a flame in a draft, before crashing to the floor behind him. The ceramic pot shattered, and dry soil crumbled on the carpet.

"What did you do that for?" demanded Arthur. "If I'd have been Real, that would have really hurt!"

"You're not real!" gasped Tom.

"No, I most certainly am not," retorted Arthur, brushing imaginary flecks of cactus dirt from his ethereal suit. "I'm Grey Arthur. I'm a ghost."

Tom's mind was whirring, desperately trying to make sense of everything. So far he wasn't having much luck. A *ghost*?

"So . . . you're dead?" asked Tom, his eyes growing wide.

"No, I'm not dead, nor have I ever been dead. I'm a ghost. It's only silly humans who think ghosts are dead people." Before quickly adding, "No offense, of course."

"You're in my bedroom."

"I know. I live here," Arthur replied, smiling enthusiastically.

"For how long?" asked Tom, his voice rising to a near-squeak.

"Oh, not long. Just over a week or so."

Tom shook his head slowly, as if trying to shake the madness out. "This is crazy."

"It's not crazy," replied Arthur. "I live here because I'm your Invisible Friend. See? Makes perfect sense."

"I don't have an Invisible Friend!"

"Well, no," agreed Arthur. "You don't now, because now you can see me. Now I suppose I'm more of a Visible Friend. It doesn't sound as good, though."

"This is crazy," repeated Tom.

"You've said that already."

"But it is! You're a ghost, but you're not dead, and you live underneath my bed, and you're my now visible Invisible Friend," said Tom slowly, as if trying to work it all out in his head. Arthur nodded in agreement as he spoke.

"That's right."

"See! Crazy." Tom heard familiar footsteps coming up the stairs, and an irrational sense of panic began. "Oh no, parents are coming. *Hide!*"

Arthur looked at Tom, confused. "Why should I hide?"

"Because," hissed Tom. "Because . . . Oh, I don't know why. Just . . . because!"

"They can't see me anyway. There's no need to hide," replied Arthur, leaning nonchalantly against the desk. There was a knock at the door—*Tap-tappy-tap-tap*—Dad's knock.

"Can I come in, Tom?" Dad asked through the door.

A look of sheer horror flashed over Tom's face, but Grey Arthur just nodded calmly. Tom tried his hardest to look normal (for some reason, he had no idea what to do with his hands, so he thrust them into his pockets, trying his best to look calm and composed).

"Uh . . . okay, sure, Dad. Come in," replied Tom, a little nervously. Arthur flashed a grin at him.

Dad nudged the door open, and wandered into the room with a sandwich in one hand and glass of juice in the other.

"Mum seemed to think you might be hungry." Dad walked over to the desk and stood right next to Grey Arthur. He placed the sandwich down, and the juice, and looked around the room. "Good to be back, Tom?" he asked.

"Yep. Yep," replied Tom. "Back to my good old, trusty, familiar room. You, er . . . you don't think there's anything different in here, then?" Grey Arthur was rolling his eyes, and just to prove to Tom that Dad couldn't see a thing he did a little tap dance right in front of him. Dad looked around the room again before his eyes settled on the photo of Tom in his school uniform, with Arthur grinning in the background.

"Ah, yes, the picture. It came out quite well in the end, don't you think?" Dad smiled approvingly at his handiwork. Grey Arthur was pulling faces at Tom's dad, and then staggering around dramatically, howling in a clichéd ghost fashion. "Oh!" said Dad, suddenly spotting something.

"What?!" demanded Tom. "What do you see?"

"You broke your cactus. I'll go get a dustpan and brush."

"Thanks, Dad," said Tom quietly. Arthur gave him his best ghostly I-told-you-so expression.

"Are you all right, Tom? You look a little pale. Maybe you should get an early night." Dad studied Tom's face, frowning.

"Do you know what, I think you're right, Dad. In fact, I'm going to bed right now. This instant." Tom nodded.

"Do you want me to send Mum up to tuck you in?" asked Dad, and Tom glanced at Grey Arthur and began to blush.

"No, I'm too old to get tucked in now, Dad."

"Fibber. You get tucked in most nights." Grey Arthur laughed.

"Shut up," Tom hissed.

"Pardon?" said Dad. "What did you just say?"

"Er . . . I, er . . . Straight up. To bed. I just want to go straight up to bed," fumbled Tom.

"Okay. Well, whatever you say. Sleep well. Just clean up the cactus in the morning if you want to get straight to sleep. Be careful not to tread on it. Good night." Dad gently shut the door behind him. Tom sank wearily onto the bed, sighing heavily. Arthur leaped onto the bed next to him, grinning.

"So, what do you want to do now? Play some games? Chat? Practice walking through walls? What is it human friends do?" Arthur bubbled enthusiastically.

"I'm going to bed. I'm going to sleep. I've had a long couple of days, and I'm convinced it's driven me stark raving mad." Tom crawled into bed fully clothed, dragging the covers up around his chin.

"Oh. Okay," replied Arthur, a little dejected. "What do you want me to do?"

"If you still exist in the morning, we'll talk about it then."

Grey Arthur got up and nodded. Crawling underneath the bed, among the old *Mr. Space Pirate* comics and the Pretty-Betsy doll, Arthur called up to Tom.

"Good night, Tom."

"Good night, Arthur."

A New Morning

THE NEXT MORNING STARTED AS ANY INCREDIBLY normal, everyday morning usually started. The alarm beeped to life, and Tom groggily reached out and turned it to snooze. Five minutes later the alarm went off again, and Tom reached out and turned it off again.

"Come on, lazybones, out of bed." Tom's mum strode into the room and pulled open the curtains, letting light stream into the room. Tom winced and rolled over, pretending to still be asleep. "No, you don't. Come on, out of bed." Tom sighed and sat up, and right up until that point everything was distinctly normal. It was then that last night's memories started trickling back into Tom's head as all the sleepiness left, and suddenly he was wide awake.

"I'm up! I'm up!" he said, hurrying Mum out of the room.

"Breakfast is on th—," she managed to say before

the bedroom door was closed. As soon as it was firmly shut, Tom ducked to the floor and peered tentatively underneath the bed.

No ghost.

No ghost!

Tom laughed with relief. Everything was okay. There were no ghosts living underneath his bed. No Invisible Friends. It was just going to be a distinctly normal, average, run-of-the-mill day. Blearily, he made his way to the bathroom, and had a normal shower, and washed his hair in a normal way (if a tad gingerly, because of the bruising), and dried himself with a normal towel, and went to put on his normal, yet garish, school uniform, quite relieved that he was a normal boy.

That is, until he found Grey Arthur floating in the wardrobe.

"Yuck, is it morning already?" Arthur yawned as Tom opened the wardrobe door. He was floating just above the floor, halfway between the shirts and the collection of shoes.

Not such a normal day.

"I couldn't sleep under the bed last night. You were sleeptalking, making an awful racket," complained Arthur, stretching. "So . . . you can still see ghosts then?"

Not such a normal boy.

"I guess so," sighed Tom.

"Excellent!" Arthur clapped. "Let's get ready for school!"

An Extra Guest at Breakfast

BREAKFAST WAS AWKWARD. MUM AND DAD WERE BUSY doing Mum and Dad things—Dad was testing out the latest version of the Anti-Static-Shock-Socks (which looked similar to the previous version, but were bright pink and with more wires sticking out) and Mum was rushing to get her uniform ironed. Grey Arthur was hovering cross-legged just above a chair, peering at the breakfast table with glee. It was very distracting. And he asked questions, *so many questions.*

"So do Mr. Space Pirate Hoops taste of pirate?"

"Are margarine and marmalade made from the same fruit?"

"Why do humans eat breakfast?"

"If you don't eat breakfast, what happens?"

"Why do your dad's socks look so stupid?"

"Why do you eat the cereal, and not the spoon as well?"

"If toasters make toast, then do ovens make ov?"

In the end Tom had to whisper, "I can't talk now. Stop asking so many questions."

He probably should have whispered more quietly, or more discreetly, because Mum noticed.

"Are you talking to yourself, Tom?" A half-amused, half-worried expression settled on her face.

"Who, me?" Tom laughed nervously. "No . . . No. I'm . . . going through my lines. For the school play."

"Really? Did you hear that, Dad?" Mum seemed very excited by this. "Our son's already got a part in the school play! Which play is it, Tom?"

"It's . . . uh . . ." Tom racked his brains. "A Shakespeare."

"Oh, I like Shakespeare," Tom's dad chipped in. "I got to play Romeo when I was at school, so if you need any acting tips you know who to come to." Dad struck up his best Shakespearean pose, the drama of which was somewhat undermined by the bright pink socks with the wires protruding from them. "Pray tell, which one art thou doing?"

"Huh?"

"Which play, Tom," replied Dad, less theatrically.

"Oh. Er . . . The one with the ghost." Tom glared at Grey Arthur, who smiled back apologetically.

"Oooh! *Hamlet*. Our son's going to be in *Hamlet*!" clucked Mum. Both parents seemed very happy with this and didn't ask any more about Tom's alleged play, which suited Tom just fine. Grey Arthur more or less behaved after that—he asked fewer questions, but he did try to eat a spoon when Tom wasn't looking, "just to see what it tasted like." Tom wolfed down breakfast as quickly as he could and bolted out the door. Grey Arthur trotted alongside him, and together, ghost and human, they headed off to school.

Side by Side

"SO, HOW COME YOU DECIDED TO START FOLLOWING me around?" asked Tom as they walked.

"You were miserable and needed a friend; I needed a job, and so I put two and two together and made an Invisible Friend. Simple, really."

"And when was this?"

"That night you got the purple eye. The night you were crying."

"I wasn't crying," lied Tom, kicking at a can on the pavement.

"Well the night your eyes were leaking water and your chin was wobbling, then."

Tom rolled his eyes. "Listen, Arthur, if you are going to insist on continuing to haunt me—"

"I prefer to call it helping," interrupted Grey Arthur.

"Fine, helping, haunting, whatever. We need to agree on some rules. I can't talk to you when other people are around, because you'll make me look crazy."

Arthur nodded.

"And no floating in my wardrobe. And no eating spoons."

"Okay," agreed Arthur.

"And I wasn't crying. I had something stuck in my eye."

"There must have been quite a big thing, because you—" Tom shot a look at Arthur, and he finally understood. "Oh, *right*. Sure."

"So that's the deal. No talking in public, no floating in wardrobes, no eating of spoons, and I wasn't crying. Okay?"

"Okay," agreed Arthur.

"Shake on it?"

Grey Arthur looked momentarily perplexed before starting to shake. His little ears waggled from side to side, his hair wobbled, and his face shuddered. Tom had to laugh.

"No . . . No. Shake on it. It's something my dad says when he seals a deal. You shake hands." He chuckled, holding out his hand.

"Oh," replied Arthur, looking a little embarrassed. "But I can't shake your hand. Ghosts can't touch humans." He reached out and grabbed the corner of Tom's sleeve instead, tugging it up and down. "Will that do?"

"Yeah, that will do." Tom smiled.

As they walked, they chatted. Tom talked about the loneliness at his new school, about the Spitting Kids, and Big Ben, and the tuft of hair he still struggled to slick down every morning. Arthur talked about his struggle to be different types of ghost, and his lonely years trying to work out what he was. Ragingly different as they were, they were similar, too, and the long, depressing walk to school didn't seem so long, or depressing, that day.

Maybe it was weird, but it also made a weird kind of sense. Grey Arthur and Tom Golden.

Tom was still finding it a little hard to adapt to being able to see and hear the ghost world, though. As they walked past a particularly nasty-smelling drain, the same stinking drain Tom had to walk past every day on his way to school, he was more than a little surprised when it swore at him.

"Did you hear that?" demanded Tom. "Did you hear what that drain just called me?"

"Don't be stupid. Drains can't talk." Arthur said, dismissing the idea. "That will be the Snorgle that lives inside it."

"A Snorgle?"

The drain swore again.

"Yes, Snorgle. A stink ghost. Most humans can smell when somewhere has a Snorgle infestation, they're just lucky enough to not be able to see or hear them. If you peered through the gratings you'd be able to see him, not that I'd recommend you do. Ugly creatures, Snorgles. Just ignore him. If you encourage him you'll just make it worse."

A rancid-sounding burp emanated from the drain.

"That's disgusting." Tom grimaced.

"If you think that's bad," said Arthur, chuckling, "you should meet the one who's moved into your boys' toilet at school. This one's positively charming compared to him."

Tom laughed. "That explains a lot, actually." They walked on awhile in silence before Tom spoke again. "It's going to take a while to get used to. Seeing ghosts, I mean. It just doesn't make much sense—I don't understand why I can see you."

"Neither do I," replied Grey Arthur. "But after school, there's someone we should go to see. She'll help us out, I'm sure. She knows pretty much everything there is to know, and a few things there aren't to know as well."

"That doesn't make any sense either." Tom sighed.

"You'll have to get used to that," said Arthur with a grin.

Visiting Mrs. Scruffles

THE SCHOOL DAY PASSED UNEVENTFULLY—WELL, AS
uneventful as a day filled with ghosts can pass. Ballpoint
Bill reluctantly handed Tom back every single pen he'd
stolen from him, although one was so badly chewed that
Tom said he could keep it. Grey Arthur managed to bribe
the boys' toilet Snorgle with a blue cheese and smoked
mackerel sandwich to follow Big Ben around all day,
which just made Tom grin from ear to ear. Tom could
smell Big Ben coming, which was useful, and watching
the other children retch and hold their noses as Big Ben
strutted through the corridor was priceless. Tom hadn't
smiled so much since he had moved house. School days
usually stretched out forever, minutes dragging past second by slow second, but today rushed toward the final
bell. Before Tom knew it, it was time to go home again.

Except Tom and Grey Arthur didn't go straight home.
Tom and Grey Arthur went to visit Mrs. Scruffles.

"This is it?" asked Tom.

"This is it," replied Arthur.

They were standing outside the old abandoned house on the corner. The same abandoned house Tom had walked past every day on his way home from school.

The old rickety gate screamed with rust as Tom pushed it open, and he gingerly stepped into the yard. Ahead led a narrow path, a tapestry of weeds, puddles, and broken tiles. The yard itself fared no better. It was overrun with brambles and stinging nettles, sticky weed, and all sorts of plants that looked as if they would scratch your skin or cling to your clothes. The grass grew long and wild. A shopping trolley, abandoned on the lawn, was being slowly covered over with ivy. Rubbish that had blown into the yard hung suspended in bushes, like strange plastic or paper fruit. The yard crawled lazily up the walls and fence, as if seeking to escape its confinement and spill out onto the streets. Tom carefully made his way through the yard, trying not to trip, or tear his trousers. The sound of crickets rattled from the long grass, and Tom was sure that many other things lived in the unruly depths of the foliage. Probably best not to think too hard about these things. . . . Nevertheless, he tucked his trousers into his socks. Just to be safe.

The house had seen better times. A window had been smashed and sloppily boarded back up again. Bent nails jutted out from the wood. The front door was buried under graffiti, and the underlying paint-work was peeling. Beneath the spray-painted words you could just about make out that the door had once been red. It wasn't cherry red, though, or fire engine red. It was a dingy-looking, nasty red. *Rash* red. The door itself hung precariously from rusting hinges.

"Go on," encouraged Arthur.

"I'm not sure I want to . . . ," whispered Tom.

Grey Arthur tutted. "Go on, trust me."

Tom pushed the door, and it creaked dramatically. Stepping over the moldy welcome mat, he held his breath and walked through the doorway. Inside, the house was . . .

Inside, the house was immaculate. Rosy pink walls stretched ahead of them into a hallway. A flurry of doilies, and potpourri, and little china ornaments gathered on shelves. A cuckoo clock, free of dust, stood boldly on a far wall. By the entrance a hand-stitched mini-tapestry gently reminded Tom and Grey Arthur to "Kindly Wipe Your Feet."

Tom looked quizzically at Arthur, who laughed.

"Appearances can be deceptive." He chuckled. Tom nodded, taking extra care to wipe his feet, in case any part of the messy garden had clung to his shoes.

"Now that's what I like to see. Good manners." A

woman breezed into the hallway, a warm smile fixed between rosy cheeks. Her grey hair was casually tussled up into a knot on her head, though a few strands had made their way free. She looked distinctly cuddly, like the kind of aunt or grandma you see on television, used to advertise toffees, or casseroles, or warm milky drinks served by a fire. As she waltzed in, Tom realized she was enveloped with a smell of baking cake, and vanilla, and sweet shops. He found himself smiling.

"Tom, this is Mrs. Scruffles. Mrs. Scruffles, Tom," said Grey Arthur, introducing the two.

"So . . . this is the human who can see ghosts?" she asked, her warm smile fixed on Tom.

"You've heard of me?"

"I have my sources. You've caused quite a stir. It's been ever such a long time since a human has been able to see ghosts. Now," she said, clapping her hands together in a jolly fashion. "Who's for a cup of tea?"

A Million Meows

MRS. SCRUFFLES LED TOM AND ARTHUR THROUGH TO the kitchen and living room, where a table had already been laid for three people. A huge teapot took pride of place in the middle of the table, and next to it was a bowl of sugar cubes, loaded so high it looked as if one false move could send umpteen crystal white lumps cascading across the table. A large grandfather clock stood proudly in the corner of the room. Several paintings hung on the wall, old watercolors, although Tom swore that the images seemed to be ever so slightly different each time he looked at them.

That wasn't the strangest thing about the room, though. Not by a long shot.

Cats.

The room was full of cats. Brimming. Cats hung from shelves, covered the settee, and entirely smothered the coffee table. Different colors, different shades, fat, thin, short haired, long haired, cats covered nearly every square inch of the space in Mrs. Scruffles's house. A constant chorus of meowing hung in the background.

"First things first. I'd best introduce you to the cats. They get terribly huffy if they think they are being ignored. This is Winston, Tabatha, Kenny, Lacey, Bels, Princess, Alfie, Iggy, Jaspar, Carrie, Cass, JJ, Charlie, Gunnersby, Dooyeb, Brontus the Third, Pumpkin, Whisky, Poppy, Ollie, Lucky, Oscar, Smokey, Puddles—you can probably work out how he got the name, the little rascal, but you can't stay mad at him for long—Stout, Ginger, Twinkle Paws, Cuddles"—a particular brutish-looking cat was pointed out here, and he looked most embarrassed—"Catnip, Furball, Tubby, Bart—Bartholomew on Sundays—Ninja, Tickles, Boo Boo, Primrose, Betty, Barney, Dumpling, Katey, Robin, and last, but by no means least, my two oldest companions: Agatha Tibbles and Carrot Cake."

Agatha Tibbles was a stout-looking Persian cat, who looked like she didn't tolerate fools kindly. She was built like a rugby player, if cats played rugby, and if cats *did* play rugby then you'd want Agatha Tibbles on your team. She meowed a hello at Tom and Arthur, and it was a deep-pitched sound. More a deep, resonating *mow* than a meow.

Carrot Cake couldn't have looked more different from Agatha. He was a scrawny, old ginger cat, with knotted hair and an eccentric look in his eye. His meow was high pitched and slightly pitiful, certainly not very masculine. He purred loudly, and it sounded like someone rattling some old kidney beans inside an empty tin can.

"Now, with the introductions out of the way, have a seat and we'll sort you out with a nice, warming cup of Earl Grey."

Mrs. Scruffles gestured for Tom and Arthur to sit down, and she began pouring out the tea into some fine china cups, cups that were detailed with tiny flowers. None of this seemed particularly ghostly. Agatha Tibbles wandered over and jumped onto Tom's lap. She felt very heavy, and warmer than a hot water bottle. He tried to pry her off, but a low rumbling growling noise persuaded him that it wasn't a good idea, and he quickly retracted his hands to a safe distance.

"Someone's taken a shine to you!" Mrs. Scruffles said, laughing. Tom nodded nervously as Agatha padded on his lap, her claws occasionally digging into his leg when she got overenthusiastic. Tom bit his lip and let Agatha get on with it.

"If you don't mind me saying, you look quite normal, for a ghost," said Tom, as he sipped his cup of tea, moving carefully so as not to disturb the very settled cat on his lap. Agatha began to purr.

"Thank you!" said Mrs. Scruffles, shooing away another cat that had decided to try and perch on the teapot. "Did you hear that, Arthur? I look *normal*." She turned to Tom and smiled. "You can come round more often!" she said as she dropped another sugar cube into his tea.

"That's a good thing, then?" asked Tom.

"Mrs. Scruffles is a Faintly Real, Tom. They're the most human of ghosts. In fact, if Mrs. Scruffles concentrates really hard, she can even appear to humans for a while. Talk to them, interact. You have to concentrate really, really hard, though, and if you don't look Real enough, humans just can't see you. They just kind of ignore you, if you aren't good enough at it. All sounds a bit too much like hard work, if you ask me."

"Grey Arthur once trained with me to be a Faintly Real," added Mrs. Scruffles. "That's how we met."

"It didn't work out, though?" asked Tom.

"It didn't work out," Arthur said, shaking his head. "Faintly Reals like doing incredibly human things, like hanging out in libraries, or in Citizens' Advice Bureaus, or supermarkets, which didn't really appeal to me. And you have to look all normal." Grey Arthur tried to straighten out his ears and failed. "Not really my thing."

"So I could have met a Faintly Real before?" asked Tom, suddenly intrigued.

"Possibly," agreed Mrs. Scruffles.

"How would I know?"

"Well . . ." Mrs. Scruffles set aside her tea and leaned in toward Tom. "Have you ever met somebody who you felt was a little strange, or odd, or not quite in synch with reality? Somebody who feels not-quite-right, but you can't put your finger on why? It could be the person who struck up the conversation with you at the bus stop, or the lady behind you in the queue at the grocer's, or the old man on the corner in all weather who waves to everyone who goes past."

Tom nodded.

"Well, there you go then, young Tom. You probably have met a Faintly Real. The only clue, the only tiny hint, is that Faintly Reals are still slightly see-through when standing in front of a light. And that," she concluded, "is why Faintly Reals avoid discos and performing onstage."

Mrs. Scruffles got up and grabbed some cookies from the cupboard. "So I really look very normal?" she asked hopefully.

"Yeah, sure," agreed Tom. "Except . . . sometimes when you walk, you forget to move your feet." Mrs. Scruffles's smile dropped, and so Tom hastily backtracked. "But that's really hardly even noticeable. I'm nitpicking. Honestly." Mrs. Scruffles's smile returned, and she set about dunking her cookie with renewed energy.

"Mrs. Scruffles is also a writer, Tom. Which is why I thought she might have some ideas about what's happening to you," said Grey Arthur, while he tried to pick a sugar cube off the top of the pile. "How many books have you written now?"

"Ninety-eight," Mrs. Scruffles replied. She knocked back an entire cup of tea in one mouthful, not even letting it touch the sides, and poured herself another.

"Ninety-eight? That's *hundreds*!" gasped Tom.

"Well, you have to bear in mind that I'm much older than your average human. Although I must admit I look good for my age. And no, I'm not saying how old I am. A lady never reveals her age."

"In other words, she's lost count," whispered Arthur, and Tom tried very hard to keep a straight face.

Mrs. Scruffles tried very hard to pretend she hadn't heard what Arthur had said.

Carrot Cake tried very hard to kill a vicious-looking teaspoon.

"So, what have you written?" asked Tom.

"Well, I don't like to brag. . . . But I'm the author of the best-selling ghost guide *A Is for Aaaaargh: The A to Z of Haunting Humans*. I suppose that would be my most popular work to date. Anyway, enough about me, yapping away when we have a real genuine human who can see ghosts in our midst!" She clapped her hands, and a notebook and pen appeared on the table before her. "Do you mind if I take notes?"

"Er . . . I suppose not," replied Tom. And so he went on and told her, in detail, about the bullying at school, the Spitting Kids and the car crash, waking up to see Arthur . . . the card signed by Ballpoint Bill, the dreams in the hospital, and all the while she took notes, nodding, and ever so often gulped down entire cups of tea and topped up Tom's and Arthur's cups. Tom had never drunk so much tea in his life. "So what do you think? Do you think the car crash made me see ghosts? When I bashed my head?"

"I don't think so, Tom." Mrs. Scruffles looked thoughtful. "You see, there was a German child once who was convinced that if he hit his head he would see ghosts. So he kept on trying, again and again, bashing his head with a plank of wood."

"What happened?" asked Grey Arthur.

"He got a little uglier, and lot stupider, and eventually one day he forgot why he kept on bashing his head in the first place. So I'm not sure it was the crash itself that made you see ghosts—if that were the case, there would be umpteen humans who could see ghosts, wouldn't there? Have you wished on a star recently, or blown out any birthday candles?"

"What? That actually works?" Tom yelped excitedly, already picturing his next birthday candle wish list. Treasure. To be a rock star. Fame and adoration! And gold! Lots of gold!

"I don't know, I was going to ask you. If you'd wished on a candle to see ghosts, and then this happened, I'd say yes. Otherwise . . . no." Tom's enthusiasm died away. "Maybe it just happened because it was meant to happen."

"That's not a very good answer." Tom sighed.

"But it might be the right one," said Mrs. Scruffles. She leaned over, picked Agatha Tibbles up off of Tom's lap, and placed her on her own. Agatha purred even louder.

"Hey, wait! You can touch cats?" Tom asked, thoroughly confused.

"Oh, Arthur, haven't you explained anything to this poor boy? No wonder he looks so confused all the time," tutted Mrs. Scruffles. Grey Arthur became incredibly interested in what Carrot Cake was doing and avoided Mrs. Scruffles's gaze. "All right, Tom, here's the abridged version," she began. "There's the Real World, and there's the Ghost World. Humans are part of the Real World, as are dogs, and gerbils, and donkeys, goldfish, flies, and most of the other animals you can think of. All the different types of ghosts: Faintly Reals, Sadness Summoners, Poltergiests, *Invisible Friends*"—she smiled at Arthur when she said that, and Arthur smiled back—"and so on, they're all in the Ghost World. Now, some things can flit between the two worlds, and just like I can occasionally appear Real and talk to humans, cats can choose whether or not they want to be Real or Ghostly, depending on their mood. We can't pick up a cat unless they decide to let us. Have you ever seen a cat stuck in a ridiculously high tree, or clinging to a telephone pole, and wondered how on earth it managed to get up there in the first place? Chances are it asked a passing ghost for a lift. They just do it for the attention." Agatha *mow*ed deeply, as if offended by that statement. "Of course, if you see a cat in an *extremely* stupid place, chances are it made the mistake of hitching a lift with a Poltergeist. Terrible practical jokers, Poltergeists . . ."

Tom was beginning to go cross-eyed. "So . . . you can pick up cats if they let you, and cats can see ghosts, but say, for example, a dog can't?"

"That's about the size of it." Mrs. Scruffles nodded.

"Dogs always do what humans tell them to do. So when humans decided ghosts didn't exist, the dogs went right along with it. Cats, however . . . Well, you can't tell a cat what to do. You can ask it, but whether it decides to or not is entirely up to it."

"Ugh. My brain hurts." Tom sighed.

"Well, it's a lot to take in at first," agreed Mrs. Scruffles.

"And ghosts *aren't* dead people?"

"Good gosh, no!" Mrs. Scruffles chuckled. "Nobody's really sure how we're made, but we certainly know how we aren't. Some ghosts are, and have always been. Some ghosts just appear one day and disappear the next. Some ghosts make ghosts, like humans can make humans."

"And Grey Arthur?" asked Tom.

"Well, Grey Arthur simply materialized one day, looking lost. And he continued looking lost for the next few centuries, didn't you, Arthur? In fact, this is the first time I've seen you look like you're not lost," she said to Arthur, who was trying to fit a spoon in his mouth sideways. "You must be doing something right."

The grandfather clock chimed the hour loudly, and all the cats meowed back at it. The sound was deafening.

"Is that four o'clock?" asked Tom.

"Five," corrected Arthur.

"Five?" Tom leaped to his feet. "Oh, Arthur, why

didn't you say? Mum and Dad are going to be wondering where I am!" Tom grabbed his schoolbag and waved at Mrs. Scruffles. "Thank you ever so much for the tea, and the explanations, of sorts. . . . I've got to dash."

"Not at all." Mrs. Scruffles smiled warmly. "It was my pleasure. And now you know where I am, you can call around anytime."

"Bub-bye, Mrs. Scruffles!" chimed Arthur, as he followed Tom out the door. "Bub-bye, cats!"

And with that the two of them bounded out of the warm house, away from the tea, and the doilies, and the multitude of cats, and back out into the overgrown yard. Tom was already halfway down the garden path by the time the front door was even shut.

"I'm so late! I'm so late! Mum and Dad are going to kill me!" he cried, and he leaped over the garden wall and began to run back home.

What Time Do You Call This?

"WHERE'VE YOU BEEN?" ASKED MUM WHEN TOM dashed in through the door. "We've been worried sick. Your dinner's gone cold as well!"

"Sorry, Mum!" cried Tom, as he hurtled up the stairs to his room. "I'll just get changed and I'll be back down."

"Don't just 'Sorry, Mum' me!" she yelled, chasing him up the stairs. "Where've you been? Why are you so late?" Grey Arthur jumped onto the bed and watched as Mum cornered Tom.

"I . . . er . . . See, the thing is . . . ," started Tom.

"Make it good," Mum said.

"I was late because when I went to go home from school, I couldn't find my locker key, and—" Grey Arthur had started waving his hands to signal Tom to stop. It was very distracting, and Tom stumbled before continuing. "And, um, where was I? Key, yes, I couldn't find my locker key, and so I couldn't get my bag out of my locker, which had my house keys in it, and so—"

"Stop it! Quick, get her out!" cried Grey Arthur, dashing around the room, as if he were looking for something. Tom stuttered, not knowing what to do.

"And so?" asked Mum.

"And so that is why I was late, because I couldn't find my keys. Good-bye now!" And he begun ushering her out of the room. Mum protested, but Tom pushed her out and shut the door. "What is it?" he hissed at Arthur, who was still frantically looking.

"You shouldn't lie like that. Your room could be bugged!" replied Arthur, rummaging on the desk.

"Quick, get me a jar or something. Quickly, *quickly*!"

Flustered, Tom picked up his pen jar from the desk and tipped all the pens out on the floor. He handed the jar obediently to Arthur. "Bugged? What do you mean, *bugged*?" Arthur put his finger to his lips and gestured for Tom to be quiet. He pointed toward an old scrap of paper on the desk.

"Oh, *nothing*, Tom. I think I was *mistaken*." He said, laboring the point, overemphasizing, and winking dramatically. Tom just stared in utter confusion—Grey Arthur was acting very strangely.

From underneath the piece of paper, a tiny ladybug crawled out and began hurrying across the desk. "Aha!" yelled Arthur triumphantly, slamming the jar down over it. "Caught you!"

"Well done," said Tom, unimpressed. "You caught a ladybug. You made me shoo my mum out of the room because of a ladybug."

"Look closer," Arthur insisted.

Tom leaned over and stared into the jar. The ladybug stood up on its back legs and waved a fist at the glass. Tom nearly leaped backward with shock. Looking closely at it, he could see it wasn't actually a ladybug at all. It was a small ghost, *dressed* as a ladybug. He had dark skin and a shock of red hair, and he was wearing a little ladybug outfit. And this little ghost was really not a happy ghost.

"What's going on? That's not fair!" he screeched

from inside the jar. He ran hard into the side of the glass and bounced harmlessly back onto the desk. "Let me out! What are you doing?"

"This," said Arthur, in his best teacher voice, "is a Bug. They work for Poltergeists."

"I don't get it. What is he doing in here?" asked Tom. The Bug was strutting around inside the over-turned jar, muttering darkly.

"There's a ghost newspaper called the *Daily Tell-Tale*. Bugs work as little minireporters. They listen out for when humans tell white lies, and they report them in the paper. You know how when you tell a white lie, like how you couldn't get your homework in on time because the printer broke? And then the next time you go to print off your homework, the printer actually is broken? Well, you've most likely been overheard by a Bug, who reported the incident in the job section. Poltergeists pick up little jobs of mischief from the job section. If we'd let this little Bug go, your locker keys would have gone missing tomorrow, and your mum wouldn't believe the same story twice now, would she?"

The Bug had given up, and he sank down to the desk, growling.

"He can't get out through the glass, can he?" asked Tom.

Grey Arthur shook his head. "Nope. Not all ghosts can pass through objects, and Bugs definitely can't.

He's stuck in there. Aren't you?" Grey Arthur tapped the glass, which sent the tiny ghost into near-spasms of rage. "Unless you promise to behave?" The Bug nodded eagerly, and so Arthur lifted the jar.

"Well, that's hardly fair now, is it?" complained the Bug. "How comes he can see me? And how comes you're helping him? A ghost helping a human, eh? What's the world coming to?"

"This is Tom Golden, and I'm his Invisible Friend. And we don't want any stories appearing about his missing locker key, okay?" said Arthur, in his best intimidating voice. It sounded just like his normal voice, only slightly deeper. It wasn't particularly intimidating.

"Fair play, I promise, no locker key story, but you're hardly playing by the rules, are you? It's not an easy job, being a Bug. It's a lot of waiting, and listening, and then finally a scoop appears in my lap, and you go and blow it for me. Do you know who I am? I'm the one, *the only*, Ladybug, and I've got a reputation to maintain, you know! So cheers. Really appreciated," he grumbled.

"So you'd just sit around, waiting for me to tell a lie?" asked Tom, scratching his head. "Can't be very interesting."

"Actually," corrected Ladybug. "You've kept me fairly busy over the years. When you moved house, I even decided to move down here with you. Follow the work, so to speak. Remember last Christmas when you lied and told your grandma that you couldn't wear that pink sweater she'd knitted you because you couldn't find it? And then it turned up on your chair, right behind you, even though you'd hidden it upstairs, and you had to wear it all day?"

"That was your fault?" spluttered Tom.

"That was me," the Bug said proudly. "And then there was the time when you said in school that you couldn't do PE because you'd forgotten your gear, and then next lesson you actually did forget your gear, but the teacher didn't believe you. Remember that? He made you wear all the leftover remnants of lost property, and you smelled like stale shoes."

"That was you too?"

"Yes, indeedy! And now, *now* I'm out of a job. Great. Fantastic. I hope you're happy, Mr. Invisible Friend." He scowled.

"Very." Arthur nodded with a grin.

"Fine. Well, I guess I'll be off then," he said, sulking, and wandered over toward the window.

"And no story about the locker key. You promised," reminded Arthur.

"Yes, yes, no story about the locker key. Bug's honor."

Just as he was about to leave, he turned and looked at Tom.

"Say fleas!" he cried, and a little light flashed out

of his hand, catching Tom at a particularly unphoto-genic moment.

"Fleas? Don't you mean cheese?" asked Tom, blinking.

"Cheese?" The Bug chuckled, fluttering toward the window. "Sure, right. Cheese!"

Tom watched him fly out of the window and pulled it shut after he'd gone.

"This ghost thing is going to take a *lot* of getting used to." He sighed.

An Expedition

THE NEXT MORNING, AS TOM AND GREY ARTHUR wandered into the history class, something was different. Instead of sitting and waiting behind the desk, Mr. Hammond stood by the door, counting heads as people came in.

"Okay, class, I hope you're all ready for your trip to the castle!"

"Castle?" asked Tom. "I completely forgot! I didn't even remember my permission slip!"

"It's okay, Tom. You handed it in already," said Mr.

Hammond, ushering Tom through the door.

"Oh, did I?" Tom said, looking at Grey Arthur, who grinned winningly back.

The last person into the room, as usual, was Big Ben. Mr. Hammond stopped him at the door.

"Ben, you're the only person who hasn't handed in a permission slip. I suppose it's too much to ask that you've brought it in today?"

"Dog ate it. Along with my homework," said Big Ben with a sneer, and some of the other kids in the class stifled laughter.

"Very original," Mr. Hammond said dryly.

From behind a history poster a tiny creature emerged. From a distance it looked like a bumblebee, and after circling once round Big Ben it flew in a haphazard fashion out of the window.

Tom burst out laughing.

"Something funny?" demanded Big Ben, glaring over at Tom from the doorway. Tom tried to keep a straight face.

"No," he said, before adding under his breath, "at least, not yet . . ." Grey Arthur giggled next to him.

"Ben, there's no need to be so aggressive," said Mr. Hammond. "Anyway, since you aren't able to come with the rest of the class to the castle without a signed permission slip, you'll have to go to the headmaster's office. Everybody else—don't bother unpacking your bags. The bus is waiting outside. Follow me!"

The bus drive took over an hour, which in bus journey time always feels like at least two. As is usually the way with school trips, all the other pupils had already decided exactly who they were going to sit next to and exactly where they were going to sit (the seats at the very back being highest in demand, as not only were they farthest away from the teachers, but they also allowed you to pull faces at the people in the cars behind). Tom had nobody to sit next to, which was all right, because it left a free seat for Grey Arthur to settle into. Tom sat right up at the front of the bus, just behind Mr. Hammond. As the bus rumbled into motion, Tom hoped that his mum stayed out of sight. Not that he didn't like his mum, not that at all, but having your mum turn up on a school trip is a bit like having your boxer shorts turn up in assembly.

The usual events occurred—a group of girls insisted on singing the same song over and over and over again, until it began to feel like someone was taking a cheese grater to your brain with every repeated, irritating verse. Someone else complained they felt sick the whole way and sat with their face buried in a plastic bag. Another kid was listening to music on his headphones, the volume so loud that you could hear a tinny rattle and the vague outline of songs, but not so loud that you could actually make out the words. Someone else had opened a packet of the smelliest cheese-and-onion crisps, ones that would make even a Snorgle's eyes water, among loud complaining from the person sitting next to him.

Tom watched all this as an observer. Nobody seemed to even notice him, which he supposed was slightly better than being given abuse, but it still felt quite wretched. In fact, if Grey Arthur hadn't been sitting next to him, chattering away, Tom would have quite easily been able to believe that it was he who was invisible, and not the ghost. Finally, after much noise and commotion, and on the sixty-third verse of "I Know a Song That Will Get on Your Nerves," Mr. Hammond's history class pulled into a car park.

The Castle

THORBLEFORT CASTLE LOOMED ON THE HORIZON, standing stark against the backdrop of fields, marshland, and sea beyond. Remnants of towers reached out like old stone fingers, scratching at the horizon. Holes in the stonework stared out like many empty eyes. Windows that once had led into rooms now led to nowhere, simply framing sections of sky, catching moving clouds like a living picture. Pigeons roosted wherever they could, taking residence in the many nooks and crannies the decrepit castle offered them. In places, whole sections stood tall and intact, stones worn smooth, green moss sprawling and ivy climbing, but every bit a castle. In other places stonework had been worn to the ground, or whole sections had been chipped away, like bite marks from a giant. The castle had a sad air about it, like a stubborn memory cling-ing to the earth, each year losing more of itself to age and the weather, and yet . . . At the same time there was something else; a feeling of history, and past, and strength, of lives and stories, pulsing through the stonework. Sad and proud, strong and broken, Thorblefort Castle stood before the pupils and waited.

"Wow," breathed Tom, staring up at the castle as he stepped off the bus. Openmouthed, he just stood for a while, taking it all in.

"I remember it when it wasn't so . . . crumbly," said Grey Arthur, floating down from the bus to Tom's side. He stared up at the castle too, a little surprised at how much had changed. "I guess it's been longer than I thought," he added, with just a hint of sadness. He shrugged. "I must have lost track of time. . . ."

"Okay, class, gather round," ordered Mr. Hammond, trying to take control of all the milling stu-dents, who had already started to disperse in different directions. Tom's mother often used the phrase "It's like herding cats!" and Tom thought it applied perfectly to this situation. "Come on, come on . . . No, don't leave your bags on the bus, take them with you. . . . Hey, you! Don't wander off yet, come back here. . . . Sally, don't do that. Put him down. . . . Okay, okay, get your pens and paper out. Have you got that little questionnaire I gave you earlier? . . . Fine, who's forgotten their questionnaire? Hands up if you've forgotten your questionnaire. . . ."

Tom rummaged in his bag and pulled out his sheet. It was your typical school-trip-type questionnaire.

(1) How old is Thorblefort Castle believed to be?
(2) What type of tree can be seen growing in the grounds of the graveyard?
(3) Make a sketch of one of the carvings seen in the stonework.

And so on. Tom took out his pen (this one even had BALLPOINT BILL—HANDS OFF! written on the side, just to make sure) and waited patiently for order to be restored.

"Come on now, it'll be time to go home at this rate. Has everyone got their questionnaire now? Everyone? Good." Mr. Hammond sighed in relief before starting his official teacher-style introduction. "Welcome to Thorblefort Castle. Built on the edge of Thorble Harbor, Thorblefort Castle, as you can probably guess from the name, was originally built as a coastal fort, although through the years it has served many purposes, from a prison to a medieval palace. This castle has sat through many wars, even received a few scars for its troubles, and has a lot of stories to tell you, if you'll only take the time to listen. Which is why we're here today—to learn about local history. Thorblefort is also rumored to be haunted, so keep your eye out for ghosts!" Mr. Hammond chuckled, and some of Tom's classmates made ghostly "Woo-ooo-ooo!" noises to one another, before falling about giggling.

"What's with the woo-ooo noises?" asked Grey Arthur, looking bemused.

"That's the noise ghosts make," whispered Tom, trying very hard not to move his lips as he talked. It's not easy having conversations with an Invisible Friend in public without looking a little bit crazy, so it paid to be discreet.

"That's ridiculous. I don't know a single ghost that makes a noise like that. That's a stupid noise," Grey Arthur retorted. He sounded most unimpressed. Tom tried to stifle a smile, but Arthur noticed. "I'm not joking! No self-respecting ghost would ever make such a stupid noise," he added, which just made Tom want to grin even more.

The school group all gathered at the base of the castle, just before the drawbridge. The moat had been emptied many years ago, and now its sloping sides were overrun with assorted greenery: huge leaves, spiky plants, and strong-smelling flowers. They were the type of slopes that, if you were to roll down them, you'd very likely be stained green until your dying day, and probably itch for a few weeks after that. Which made Tom want to roll down them even more.

"Okay, class, we're about to enter the castle, so if we could all stick together, please? No wandering off just yet. We'll go around the different rooms together, and then you'll have some time to do some sketches, have some lunch, and have a look round on your own before we go home. Is everybody clear on that? Any questions? No? Good. Okay, class, follow me!" Mr. Hammond waved the class on, and everyone began to march forward, across the drawbridge and into the castle beyond.

Faster Than a Speeding Gossip

GREY ARTHUR HADN'T THOUGHT TO WARN TOM. After all, to a ghost, a castle is a very normal thing indeed, and it had slipped his mind that it might, just *might,* help to have told Tom that the place would be flooded with ghosts. Though, to be fair to Grey Arthur, even he was taken aback by what happened next.

Because Grey Arthur hadn't been reading the *Daily Tell-Tale.*

Ladybug had been true to his word—the story of Tom's missing locker key had been kept from the paper, and in turn from the Poltergeists. Ladybug had promised not to write a story on Tom's Little White Lie, and so he hadn't.

Instead the *Daily Tell-Tale* led with the exclusive headline: REVEALED! THE HUMAN BOY WHO CAN SEE GHOSTS!!

There had been a few errors in the article—they called Tom Golden "Tom Goujon," and said he was eleven months old, instead of eleven years old, and stated that he started seeing ghosts after being hit by a *star* and not a car, but to the ghosts these small details didn't really matter. What did really matter was that finally, after all these long endless years, there was a human who could appreciate their ghostliness. A human who could marvel at their headless horseman act, tremble at their chain rattling, gasp at their ability to run through walls while screaming. At the end of the article, Ladybug had helpfully written that Tom was going to be "doing a guest appearance at Thorblefort Castle," adding the exact date and time (he'd snuck back later that night and gone through Tom's mum's diary). So if Grey Arthur had read the *Daily Tell-Tale* like every good ghost does, he'd know that ghosts from all over England would be traveling down to see the Human Boy Who Can See Ghosts. If Grey Arthur had read the *Daily Tell-Tale,* he could have warned Tom. Instead Grey Arthur had taken to reading *Mr. Space Pirate* comics instead, and so was blissfully unaware of what waited . . .

Over the Drawbridge

TOM WALKED ONTO THE CASTLE GROUNDS AND ground to a halt. His feet just stopped working, his mouth dropped open, and while everyone else in his class was filing past, oblivious, Tom stood stock-still and stared in shock.

"Come along, Tom, don't dawdle," said Mr. Hammond.

"Mepywhjrrs . . . ," said Tom. It was meant to be a word, in theory, but all that came out was a tangle of noises.

"Tom?"

Pure insanity bubbled within the confines of the castle walls. *Hundreds* of ghosts were waiting for Tom—some had even stayed overnight in order to guarantee getting the best haunting positions. Some had no heads and just stood there, striking dramatic yet headless poses, waiting to be noticed, or walked along, occasionally stumbling, hands sweeping out in front of them like someone playing blindman's buff. Some were draped in reams and reams of old chains and shook them theatrically at Tom. Snorgles gathered around the bins, strange eyes glinted from the shadows, mildly see-through ghosts danced beatific dances on the walls or leaned out of the tower windows, waving. Thespers, the ghostly equivalent of actors, marched across the battlements or pranced across the courtyard, recreating historical events. One very melodramatic Thesper, clutching an ethereal bunch of wilting flowers, was shouting a lament for a lost soldier. When she realized she was being upstaged by a Chain Rattler shaking practically an entire scrap-metal yard's worth of chains, she started the entire speech again, only louder and with bigger gestures. The Chain Rattler responded by shaking his chains harder and adding an additional spooky noise.

"Whoops," said Grey Arthur, in a case of monumental understatement.

"Whoops?" Tom repeated, eyes wide, still trying

not to move his lips. He spoke like a poor ventrilo-quist. "What on *earth* is going on?"

A Headless ran up to Tom, head in his hands. He thrust his head toward Tom, and it shouted something very ghostly and poignant before he was shoved aside by a Faintly Real desperate to show off his human impression. He'd forgotten to have nostrils, which was a minor flaw that paled into insignificance when compared with the fact that he was at least eight feet tall and his feet were the size of large concrete blocks. Tom tried to smile politely, but his mouth was so dry that his top lip just clung to his gums and stayed there. Some of the ghosts were forming an orderly queue to get to Tom now, and the Faintly Real was soon replaced by a Thesper, overenunciating an old battle speech while dressed in an ancient, dusty military uni-form.

"Come on, Tom, what's the matter with you? Have you never seen a castle before?" called Mr. Hammond. The rest of the class was waiting for Tom to catch up. "And if you don't shut your mouth, you'll catch flies." Tom clamped his mouth shut, and his lip sprang free from where it had stuck.

"Just ignore them, Tom," Arthur advised, swatting away a persistent Chain Rattler. "Just keep on walk-ing. I'll try to sort this out." Tom nodded dumbly.

Ignoring them was easier said than done. With the whole of the school party watching and waiting, he tried his hardest to concentrate and just walk forward. No weaving between the hordes of ghosts, no side-stepping, just in a straight line as if there were no ghosts in his way, like a normal person would walk. He took a deep breath and stepped forward.

"Forth, forth my soldiers! Out into the fray!" cried the military Thesper as Tom marched determinedly through him. Colors flashed across Tom's eyes, and for a brief moment it felt strangely cool, like the sun had just disappeared behind a cloud. When he stepped out the other side of the Thesper (who seemed quite indignant at being walked through), everything immediately warmed up again. Tom had never knowingly walked through a ghost before—Grey Arthur was always polite enough to step aside—but it did make him wonder just how many he might have walked through by accident before he was able to see them.

With each step Tom picked up momentum, walking with gritted teeth straight through the crowds of ghosts. Some would dive out of his way, some would determinedly stand their ground, and some even dived in front of Tom in order to be walked through. Tom tried his hardest not to flinch.

The pupils, wandering around in circles waiting for Tom to catch up, acted as if nothing was amiss. They walked through ghosts as if they weren't even there, which of course, to them they weren't. Occasionally they would shiver a little, and say that it felt like someone had walked over their grave, but mostly they were blissfully unaware of the multitude of ghosts that surrounded them. Which was just as well, really.

Tom finally caught up with his class and smiled triumphantly. "I made it!" he said, which sparked off giggling from some of the other kids.

"I never had any doubt," said Mr. Hammond, ushering Tom back with the rest of the class.

"You go ahead, Tom!" Grey Arthur cried from the middle of the courtyard. He was trying to herd all the ghosts into one corner. "I'll have a word with these ghosts out here. Find out what's happening."

Tom put his hand behind his back and flicked a thumbs-up sign in the direction of Arthur before filing into the castle with the rest of the group.

"Right!" shouted Arthur at the top of his voice. "Can somebody *please* tell me what's going on?"

The Price of Fame

GREY ARTHUR STUDIED THE COPY OF THE *DAILY TELL-Tale* that had been handed to him by the nostril-less

Faintly Real. There was a picture of Tom on the front cover, looking particularly daft.

"Could you get him to sign it for me?" asked the Faintly Real.

"Sorry, what?" Grey Arthur asked, scratching his hair, distracted by the newspaper. A Ladybug exclusive, huh? And no mention of Grey Arthur at all!

"Could you get Tom Goujon to sign my copy of the *Daily Tell-Tale*?" he asked again.

"Er, sure. Well, I'll ask him. I'm not sure how good a mood he's going to be in after today." Grey Arthur folded away the newspaper and crammed it into his pocket. It wouldn't have fit, not if it had been a real newspaper, nor if it had been a real pocket, but luckily it was neither. "You shouldn't have crowded him like that. It was a bit overwhelming."

The military Thesper snorted. "It's been more years than I care to count since we've been able to perform in front of a human properly. They used to love that speech. . . . I'd stand on the battlements, late at night, always when the moon was at its thinnest, and I did that same speech once a month for well over a century." He stared into the distance, reminiscing. "Even performed in front of royalty once. King Henry the Something or Other turned pale as a sheet, and I swear he would have run away if his legs hadn't been so round. Then suddenly, a snap of the fingers and they can't see us anymore." He looked back at

Grey Arthur. "You can't blame us for getting excited."

"Anyway," added a Chain Rattler at the back of the crowd, "how come you're allowed to haunt him, and we're not?"

There were many assorted murmurs of agreement at that.

"I'm not haunting him!" replied Grey Arthur, shaking his head. "I'm his Invisible Friend."

"An Invincible Fiend? Sounds sinister!" said the military Thesper, intrigued.

"No, no. *Invisible Friend,*" corrected Arthur.

"What on earth does an Invisible Friend do?" asked another Faintly Real.

"Well, I follow this human around all day and—" Grey Arthur started, before being interrupted.

"Force-feed him nightmares?" asked one ghost.

"Drink his fear?" asked another.

"Chew away his sanity like a dog chews on a bone?" volunteered a very dusty-looking Chain Rattler.

"Er . . . No. No, not quite," replied Grey Arthur. "I help him out. Little things, like taking notes off his back, or making sure he doesn't forget his packed lunch."

There was an awkward silence, punctuated by the occasional chink of chains.

"There's more to it than that, though," Arthur continued, seeing all the confused faces. "We're

138

friends. We keep each other company. We talk, and we laugh, and I stop him from being miserable. If he's having a bad day, then I try to make it better. He smiles a lot more now, which is great, and to be honest, I'm a lot happier too. It's nice finally finding out what you are, instead of what you aren't."

"Each to his own, I suppose," commented the military Thesper, after a long, drawn-out pause. "As long as it keeps you busy."

"Oh, it certainly does that." Grey Arthur grinned before changing the subject. "So all of you traveled all the way down here just to meet Tom?"

"Some of us already lived here," said a nearby Headless, his head tucked securely under his arm. "But most of the ghosts here are tourists. Some have come from miles and miles away too."

A tiny Faintly Real chipped in enthusiastically. "We even had a Screamer come down all the way from the Outer Hebrides! It's been a long time since this castle's had a Screamer. . . ."

"Th-there's a Screamer?" stammered Grey Arthur.

"There most certainly is— Hey, where are you going?" the Headless cried, as Grey Arthur pushed past him. Grey Arthur didn't respond, he just forced his way through, frantically trying to get to Tom. Other ghosts clustered around him, asking questions, demanding to see the Human Boy Who Can See Ghosts, wanting to know how Tom and Arthur met, and Grey Arthur had to wade through them all, slowing his progress to a crawl.

"Please!" he shouted above the noise. "Please let me through! I have to get through!" But if the other ghosts heard him, they didn't seem to pay much attention. Grey Arthur moved relentlessly forward, elbows digging into those that weren't fast enough in getting out of his way, but it was painfully slow work.

"I'm coming, Tom," he breathed, as he managed to move forward another few meters.

He only hoped that he got there in time.

Among the Shadows

"AND THIS ROOM," INTONED MR. HAMMOND IN HIS best theatrical voice, "would have been the dungeon."

It was very dark in the lower parts of the castle. What little light filtered through the upper windows seemed to be smothered by shadows as soon as it entered the room, and there was an overwhelming smell of damp. The class had all been ushered inside, and it was as if everyone had become strangely muted—voices were automatically more hushed, and even the most hyperactive of pupils were unnaturally still. The dungeon just didn't feel like the type of room you messed around in.

"What we're going to do in here, class, is take a little time to do some etching. If you look carefully at the walls, you will see some very early examples of graffiti. Where prisoners would have been kept for years, they carved their names and the dates into the stonework, as a lasting reminder of what they had been through. What I want you to do is to get your questionnaires, and I've left a page blank for you to put over the graffiti and take an etching of what is carved there. It shouldn't take more than a few minutes, and when you're done, come up and join me upstairs in the churchyard. Everybody clear?"

There was a faint muttering of "yes" from the class.

"Good. I'll see you in a few minutes then," said Mr. Hammond, climbing the spiral staircase out of the dungeon.

While the rest of the class paired up or formed groups to makes etchings, Tom retreated quietly to a corner and, finding a suitable engraving to copy, placed his paper against the wall and began to color in the sheet. It was nice to be away from all the ghosts, and as Tom scratched the pencil against the paper, watching the outline of writing appear on it, he lost track of time. When he turned round to look at how everyone else was doing, he realized he was alone.

Nobody had even bothered to nudge him as they left. Tom quickly finished off the etching and stood up to leave.

Which was when the room got darker.

The shadows that sprawled across the floor of the dungeon seemed to be stretching, growing, spilling out across the room. Tendrils of darkness contorted and warped, crawling across the masonry like greedy hands. A cold fear gripped Tom, and he retreated into the corner, back pressed against the wall. The far corner of the dungeon was getting darker, and darker, until it was just a mass of writhing black. Tom glanced across at the way out, and it seemed a long way away, and he wasn't even sure he could run if he wanted to. A horrid fear locked him in place. He pushed himself harder against the wall, back flat, instinctively recoiling from what was in front of him.

From the darkest corner of the dungeon something moved. It stretched, clicking old bones into place, and stood up, before beginning to walk toward Tom, curled toenails clicking on the floor with every step. It looked like someone had haphazardly stitched some shadows together, stretched taut over a skeletal frame, and it had a smile like broken glass thrown into a puddle of oil. As it breathed, it sucked light out of the room and exhaled shadows in its place. Its eyes, if you could call them that, were rough indentations in the face, where pools of mist gathered, swirling mesmerizingly. These "eyes" were fixed on Tom. It tilted its head, as if studying him.

Tom realized he hadn't remembered to breathe, and he gulped in a mouthful of air. His mouth was dry as dust.

The Screamer stalked forward slowly, the constant sound of clicking toenails just audible over the sound of Tom's heart hammering in his ears. Its arms were scrawny, sinewy, and its fingernails were so long they had begun to curl in different directions. It stopped roughly a meter in front of Tom, jagged smile widening. Shadows seeped out from around where it stood, oozing across the floor toward Tom. He tried to edge farther back, going up on tiptoe to retreat from the tide of black that was flowing toward him, but there was no space left. Shadows lapped at his feet and began to crawl up his legs, twining around his trousers. Tom wanted desperately to shake them off, but his legs refused to move. Coldness seeped through the material of his trousers wherever the shadows touched. Tom's breathing was ragged, tiny gasps, and he was unable to tear his eyes away from the whirling mist eyes sunk into the ghost's face. The ghost leaned in closer to Tom, sniffing the air like an animal, its smile widening.

And then it screamed.

Tom screamed right back.

And then he fled. His legs just started running, before his mind had even caught up. He bolted toward the exit, screaming all the while, and threw himself up the stairs, a mad scramble of hands and feet. He didn't dare look back, didn't dare turn round in case *that thing* was behind him, and so he pushed himself on, tumbling over his own feet in his haste to get away. It felt like the shadows were chasing him upward, curling around the staircase as he ran, and this spurred him on faster, faster, twisting up the spiral staircase. Some shadows still clung to his trousers, torn shreds of black, and with clumsy hands he frantically brushed them off as he ran. He tumbled out into the open air and light (how glad he was to be in the light), skidding to a halt in front of all the waiting class. The remaining shadows on Tom vanished as soon as they were hit with sunlight, fading away to nothing, but still he could feel the cold touch where they had been.

"Ah, there you are, Tom, we were just about to send someone down looking for you . . . ," Mr. Hammond said, before he realized how terrified Tom looked. "Are you all right, Tom? You look like you've seen a ghost!"

Just then Grey Arthur sped round the corner and screeched to a halt.

"Tom, are you okay?" he asked, looking concerned. "I got here as soon as I realized."

"Ghost!" Tom gasped, his eyes wide, pointing down toward the dungeon. The other kids stared at Tom as if he were deranged.

Both Grey Arthur and Mr. Hammond answered him at the same time.

"It's okay, Tom, it was probably just someone playing a harmless prank on you," said Mr. Hammond.

"It's okay, Tom, I know they look terrifying, but really they're harmless," Grey Arthur said.

"*Harmless?*" repeated Tom, still struggling for breath. It certainly hadn't looked harmless.

"Harmless." Grey Arthur nodded. "Trust me, I used to share a room with one."

"Yes, harmless. Just someone's poor idea of a joke." Mr. Hammond nodded.

Tom burst out laughing, and if you asked him he wouldn't be able to tell you exactly why. Maybe it was the absurdity of the ghost and the teacher answering him both at once, maybe it was the relief of escaping from that terrifying thing in the dungeon, maybe it was both of these things and maybe it was neither, but Tom laughed so loudly he startled the pigeons, who all began to fly away.

Mr. Hammond looked nervously at Tom. "Are you okay?" he asked. Some of his classmates nudged one another and whispered behind cupped hands, but Tom didn't care.

"I'm fine." He chuckled. "I'm fine."

"Okay then, well, come and join the rest of the class. We're just about to have a final talk about the old cemetery on the grounds of the church, and then everyone's splitting up for lunch. Right, listen up, everyone! I want you to take a look at this glorious old yew tree that stands on the grounds of the cemetery. Yew trees are commonly found in . . ."

Laughter continued to bubble inside Tom, and the more he tried to hold it in, the more it came. His shoulders shook, and his eyes watered, and still he laughed. Marianne stared at Tom, her eyebrows scrunched in disgust. "What is *wrong* with you? You're such a freak."

It just made Tom laugh harder. She turned on her heel, back to him, and Tom could hear her group of friends talking, deliberately within earshot.

"What a weirdo."

"I know! I don't get why he's laughing. He's so strange. And did you see the look on his face when he ran up those stairs?"

"He gives me the creeps. Do you know he talks to himself as well sometimes?"

"Really?"

"Seriously. I've seen him do it."

Kate turned her head and looked at Tom over her shoulder. "You're so pathetic, Tom."

The girls all laughed at that and walked off after Mr. Hammond, arms linked. Tom trotted behind them, still chuckling to himself.

"Are you sure you're okay, Tom?" asked Arthur, frowning. "It must have been quite scary, if you've never seen a Screamer before. You're definitely okay?"

"I'm fine, honestly. I've just got the giggles."

Arthur nodded, not really understanding. Tom's laughter was finally subsiding, still there but quieter, and every now and then he would shake his head, smiling to himself. Mr. Hammond was *still* talking about the same yew tree, leading the class in circles around it, saying how to work out its age, and what a marvelous specimen it was, all of which was greeted with great indifference by the class, which had gotten bored a good few minutes ago. All of a sudden Tom stopped in his tracks. The laughter vanished that second, just as if someone had flipped a switch, and Tom tilted his head, as if listening to something that nobody else could hear.

"Tom?" said Arthur. "Tom, what's going on?"

Tom didn't respond. He looked around, trying to work out something, and then began to walk away from the class, marching through the cemetery. Mr. Hammond saw Tom breaking away from the group and called out to him.

"Tom, where are you wandering off to now? Tom? *Tom!*"

Tom didn't even turn his head. A song fluttered on the air, distracting him, calling him, and he had to find where it was coming from. He couldn't ignore it— this song, this beautiful song, danced around his ears and blocked out everything else. He stumbled along, following the thread of the music, and right there and then, nothing else mattered.

Then he saw her.

There was somebody sitting on the cemetery wall, and once Tom had seen her, he felt like he couldn't look away. She was sitting with her back to him, and he couldn't see her face, but he knew beyond a shadow of a doubt that this song belonged to her. Grey Arthur stood in front of Tom, trying to say something, but Tom just walked straight through him, not even noticing. He had to get closer to her. To the song.

As he approached, and could see her better, the song grew around him until he could practically feel it against his skin. It felt like he imagined dew would feel, settling in the early morning.

Her hair was long and tangled, and the color of cold winter moonlight. It fell down to her waist, twisting and curled like the path of a river, and dusky jewels embedded in her hair glinted palely. Her dress was the darkest blue, darker than midnight, and deep within the fabric lights flickered and then disappeared, like distant stars dying. The long dress fell into tatters at the bottom, the beautiful material trailing into ragged threads just above her bare feet. Her skin was also blue, beautiful blue, ice blue, poison blue, drowning blue . . .

And that song, that song dragged Tom forward like the tide drags the sea. . . .

It was an old language, history and stories woven into words so old that their original meaning had been lost, and all that remained were the glittering threads of sorrow that wove the words into song. It sounded like water, like streams of silver, like crystals and tears and moonlight. Tom drifted toward her, mesmerized by the beautiful song made from forgotten words. Somewhere at the back of reality, he could hear the teacher calling him, and he could hear Grey Arthur begging him to stop, to not look at her, to turn away, but with every note she sang everything else became fainter and fainter, and with each clumsy step toward her the song grew around him, so strong that he felt sure that if he were to close his eyes he would even be able to see it.

When he was almost close enough to reach up and touch her, she slowly, slowly turned her head, her beautiful hair tumbling like a waterfall, sensing he was nearby. That song still on her lips, she turned and looked at Tom.

Tom looked back.

He looked into those eyes, those beautiful eyes of ice and marble and bitter dreams, and every tear he had ever cried, every sadness he'd ever felt threw itself back at him tenfold. He fell to his knees, huge gulping sobs racking his body, tears streaming down his face, crying so hard he was gulping for breath, and Sorrow Jane, the Sadness Summoner, sang on, that haunting song of forgotten words tied together with grief, her eyes swimming with century-old tears.

Distantly Tom was aware of Grey Arthur at his

side, screaming at Sorrow Jane. He was faintly aware of Mr. Hammond crouched next to him, his voice heavy with worry. At the back of reality, he realized when his mother arrived, running from the castle tea shop, apron still on, now holding him tightly, and he was aware of the other children, staring, being ushered away. All this was pushed to the back of his thoughts, because everything else was drenched in tears.

He was helped to his feet, and Mum and Mr. Hammond helped take him to Mum's car. Grey Arthur walked alongside him, trying to talk to him, to break him free of the tears, but he was still sobbing heavily, his eyes red. He sat in the car, and Grey Arthur sat beside him, his ghostly face all etched with worry.

"I'm so sorry," he said, over and over again. "I'd never have let you go if I'd known she was going to be there. I'm so sorry." But Tom could only look ahead, tears streaming down his face.

Mum was allowed to leave work early, and she drove Tom straight home. Hundreds of ghosts lined the exit to wave good-bye to Tom, but he didn't even notice.

The farther they got from the castle, the more distance between Tom and that song, those eyes, the better he felt, the more the tears subsided, but a heavy sadness still clung to him like grey clouds cling to the sky. When they were nearly home they drove past a boy chasing a dog down the street. As they got closer

Tom could see it was Big Ben, and the dog seemed to have its mouth crammed full of paperwork. Big Ben's face was red with rage, and each time he'd make a grab for the dog it would gleefully race ahead, just out of reach. Normally, this scene would have Tom in near-hysterics, but now he just watched it all with red, aching eyes, and he couldn't even muster a smile. By the time they pulled up outside the house, there was no more crying. Tom's head was pounding, though, and his throat was sore.

"I'm sorry to cause such a fuss, Mum," he whispered.

"Not at all, Tom. Not at all," she said, helping him out of the car. Her lips were thin, and she looked very serious. No smiles. She placed her hand against his forehead, feeling for a temperature, and frowned when there wasn't one. "Let's just get you in and up to bed."

"I'm fine, Mum, honestly. I feel a lot better now. I just had a funny five minutes," protested Tom weakly. "Please don't be worried."

"I'm not worried," said Mum, even though everything about her screamed that she was. "Just go upstairs and have some rest, and we'll see if you're feeling any better when Dad comes home from work. I've phoned him, and he'll be back soon. Okay?"

Tom nodded feebly, and Mum escorted him up to bed. Grey Arthur followed and perched on the edge of his desk.

"I don't want to go to bed, Mum, it's the middle of the day."

Mum nodded, but Tom knew she wasn't going to give any ground on this. She handed him two headache tablets and a glass of water.

"Take these, have a lie-down. If you still want to come downstairs in a bit, then you can, but I don't want you overdoing it."

Tom sighed but did as she asked. She felt his head again and then left, drawing the curtains and dimming the lights on her way out.

"Are you okay?" asked Arthur, jumping down from the desk and coming over to sit on the bed. "I had no idea Sorrow Jane was there, none at all. I'm really, *really* sorry."

"I don't want to do this anymore," said Tom, shaking his head and rubbing at his bloodshot eyes.

"Do what?"

"This! See ghosts. I don't like it anymore. Whatever happened, I want to undo it."

"You don't mean that. You've just got some left-over misery from seeing a Sadness Summoner. That happens, it's normal."

"I do mean it! And this is far from normal!" replied Tom, rubbing at his forehead with the palm of his hand. "Do you have any idea how embarrassing today was for me? Not only do I run into the whole entire class looking terrified, but then I laugh like a complete lunatic, and then I burst into tears and everyone sees, and *then* my mum has to take me home. You have *no idea* how awful that is."

"I know that you're upset. I can hear it in your voice," Arthur said gently. "And I know today must have been horrible for you."

"I just want to be a normal kid. I want to fit in, and have friends, and not get gum spat in my hair, and not get threatened with broken bottles, and not burst into tears when I go to castles," said Tom, pulling the duvet up around him. "I don't want to be Freak Boy. I just want to be normal. And seeing ghosts *isn't* normal."

"But if you couldn't see ghosts, then you couldn't see me," said Arthur quietly.

"I know, Arthur, and I don't want that, but at the same time . . . Oh, I don't know! This is just all very hard to take in. Maybe I do need to have a rest. I've got an awful headache." He lay his head down on the pillow. Arthur nodded and stood up.

"I'll let you get some sleep then. See if you feel better afterward. I'll be under the bed if you need me."

"Thanks, Arthur," Tom said, turning on his side. "And, Arthur? You are a really good friend. I mean that. It's just . . ." He trailed off into silence. He didn't need to finish what he was saying, though. Grey Arthur understood.

"Get some rest," he said, crawling underneath the bed.

And within thirty seconds, Tom was fast asleep.

A One-Sided Conversation

"HE'S UPSTAIRS, RESTING," SAID MUM, AS DAD CAME in the door. "I just really don't know what's going on. He was distraught when I got there, absolute floods of tears. To be honest, it scared me."

"Well let's go up now and check on him, see if he's feeling any better," Dad said, putting his coat on the banister. They walked up together, footsteps light, avoiding the creaky steps in case Tom was asleep. Tiptoeing, they approached the door, and as they got closer Dad frowned.

"Has he got someone in there with him?" he asked in a whisper. Mum shook her head and mouthed, "Why?" Dad gestured for her to lean in closer, and together they pressed their ears against Tom's door.

". . . and everyone sees, and *then* my mum has to take me home. You have *no idea* how awful that is."

There was silence from the room before Tom spoke again.

"I just want to be a normal kid. I want to fit in, and have friends, and not get gum spat in my hair, and not get threatened with broken bottles, and not burst into tears when I go to castles. I don't want to be Freak Boy. I just want to be normal. And seeing ghosts *isn't* normal."

Another pause.

"I know, Arthur, and I don't want that, but at the same time . . . Oh, I don't know! This is just all very hard to take in. Maybe I do need to have a rest. I've got an awful headache."

Mum and Dad exchanged worried glances and quietly crept back downstairs.

BOOK THREE

* * * * * * *

Strictly Between You and Me

Sitting in Silence

TOM DIDN'T GO INTO SCHOOL THE NEXT DAY. IT WASN'T discussed or decided upon, but when Tom's alarm went off in the morning and, as usual, he turned it off to get a few more minutes' sleep, nobody came in to cajole him out of bed. There was no tearing open of the curtains, no morning light pouring into the room, no "Come on, lazybones." Tom sank back into deep sleep, uninterrupted, and even Grey Arthur let him be.

When he woke up it was nearly midday, and the sun was high up in the sky. He peered underneath the bed, but Grey Arthur wasn't there. Stretching, he got out of bed and wandered downstairs, still in his paja-mas. He was sporting bed hair, and his face still had creases in it from the pillow.

Dozily he pushed open the door into the kitchen. Grey Arthur was perched up on the kitchen counter, looking a bit concerned. At the table were his mum and dad, and a third person sat with them. He looked teacher age, but he wasn't dressed like a teacher. He wore a heavy knit V-neck sweater in tangles of woolly brown, and beneath that he wore an old-fashioned shirt, finished off with a novelty tie. Tom squinted at it, rubbing the sleep from his eyes, and could just about make out pictures of tiny bears juggling. At his side was a battered leather briefcase, and on the table he had a notepad and a pen. He'd written notes on the paper, and Tom quickly read "Talking to invisible friend—query ghost?" at the top before the man noticed Tom looking and shut the book.

"Who's this?" Tom asked.

The stranger stood up and extended a hand for Tom to shake. He smiled warmly.

"Well, you must be Tom. I'm Dr. Brown."

Tom didn't shake his hand.

"I already told Mum last night. I'm not sick. I just had a funny five minutes, that's all. I don't need a doctor."

There was a brief, uncomfortable silence. Mum tugged at her hair, and Dad stared intently into his cup of tea. Dr. Brown just wore the same unflinching smile, and took away the hand he'd left for Tom to shake, instead adjusting his tie.

"He's not that kind of doctor, Tom," Dad said softly, finally looking up. Tom looked at his parents, confused.

"I don't understand."

"It's okay, I'll explain," said Dr. Brown, gesturing

toward a chair at the table. "Do you want to take a seat, Tom?"

"Not particularly. I just want to know what's going on." Something about all this made Tom feel deeply uneasy. Grey Arthur was uncharacteristically quiet, staring at the floor, swinging his legs over the edge of the kitchen worktop.

"I'm an expert on treating children who, well . . . How to phrase this? Children who believe they can see things that other people can't see. Children who have, for example, imaginary friends," Dr. Brown said, stooping slightly to get eye contact. Tom laughed nervously.

"Imaginary friends? I don't know what you're talking about!" His pulse quickened. "I'm *far* too old to having imaginary friends. I'm not a kid."

"It's okay, Tom," said Dad, in his best reassuring voice. The voice he used to use when Tom was younger, for nightmares, or stormy nights, or for the fear that something was beneath the bed. "We know."

Tom's mouth dried.

"We've heard you. Yesterday. Talking in your room," added Mum. "We just want to help."

"I don't need help," interrupted Tom, but Mum continued in a calm, measured voice.

"We found Dr. Brown on the Internet. He's a leading expert on the subject."

"If I do say so myself." Dr. Brown grinned. His teeth

161

were off-white, and his breath smelled of something familiar, and it took Tom a while to place it . . . aniseed balls. Tom cringed, and recoiled slightly. Aniseed balls are small, spherical, hard-boiled sweets that you either love, relishing their medicinal flavor, or you hate, desperately wishing after a taste that you could remove your tongue from your mouth and put it in a washing machine for an hour, just to get the lingering aniseedness out of your mouth. Tom was a long-established member of the hating group. He says that they taste like death. Not that he's ever tasted death, but he's sure that if he ever did, it would taste like aniseed balls.

Tom realized everyone was waiting for a response, but he didn't say anything. He just looked at his parents, then at the sincere-looking Dr. Brown, then at Grey Arthur perched on the worktop trying to blend in with the tea and coffee containers. There was so much he wanted to say, so many denials, a smattering of white lies, a few angry accusations—why had his parents been listening in on him?—but in the end he just turned and ran out of the kitchen, and up the stairs, and into the shelter of his bedroom, slamming the door shut behind him.

Grey Arthur leaped through the door just a few seconds later, but he knew better than to say anything. He just sat beside Tom on the bed, and they didn't talk or even look at each other, but simply sat in heavy silence, wondering what would happen now.

An Unfamiliar Knock

A FEW MINUTES LATER THERE WAS A KNOCK AT THE door. It wasn't Mum's knock, and it wasn't Dad's knock, so Tom knew it had to be this Dr. Brown man from downstairs, but he asked anyway. "Who is it?"

"It's Dr. Brown. Can I come in?" came a muffled voice.

"What does it say on the door?" asked Tom.

"It says 'Keep out, by order of Tom Golden,'" replied Dr. Brown.

"Well then. There's your answer." Tom lay back on the bed, head resting on the pillow.

"Maybe you should let him in," said Grey Arthur softly.

"I can't believe they've done this to me. I'm not a child anymore. I don't need some stupid kiddie doctor talking to me like I'm daft, or crazy, or both. They shouldn't have been listening in on me anyway." He looked at Arthur, eyebrows scrunched together in a worried scowl. "What were they talking about down-stairs? Before I came down. What were they saying?" Tom was whispering, not wanting Dr. Brown to hear through the door. Grey Arthur sighed.

"They're just worried, Tom. After the car smashing into you, and you going a little strange at the castle—"

"That wasn't my fault!" interrupted Tom, forgetting

to keep his volume under control. "That wasn't my fault," he repeated more quietly.

"I know, I know it wasn't. But they don't. They're just concerned. I think they're worried that you might still be a little broken after your accident."

Tom made a noise, a sound halfway between a sigh and a growl, while holding his face in his hands. Grey Arthur wasn't sure what to make of this, and so he just waited patiently for Tom to stop. Dr. Brown knocked at the door again.

"Tom?" he asked. "Tom, are you okay? Can I come in?"

Tom sat up on the bed. "Okay, I'm going to let him in," he whispered to Arthur. "But you have to behave. No distracting me, and no smart comments. I have to appear very, *very* normal. I just need to get rid of him, convince him I'm fine. Okay?"

"I promise. Ghost's honor. I'll be good as gold," said Grey Arthur, and he crawled into the corner of the bed, against the wall, and sat very still. He concentrated, put on a serious expression, straightened out his hair and ears, and even tried to look a little less fuzzy and see-through. "I'm ready when you are."

Tom got up and flung open the door, revealing Dr. Brown stooped outside with his ear pressed to the woodwork. He blushed and stood up, straightening his tie.

"Come on in," Tom said.

Honesty Is the Best Policy

TOM SAT BACK ON THE EDGE OF THE BED, LEAVING DR. Brown to sit on Tom's rickety old chair at the desk (Tom always leaned back in it, putting all the weight on the back two legs, and the chair looked as if any day now it would collapse, just to teach Tom a lesson). Dr. Brown didn't look at all confident sitting in it, and he perched as if trying to balance his weight. He smiled at Tom, but Tom didn't feel much like smiling back.

"Okay, Tom, before we talk I want you to know that everything we discuss here is said in the strictest confidence, meaning it won't go any farther than this room." He popped an aniseed ball into his mouth and offered a crushed paper bag full of sweets to Tom. "Aniseed ball?"

"No, thanks," declined Tom. "I don't like them."

"All the more for me then." Dr. Brown grinned, pushing the bag back into his trouser pocket. "Anyway, as I was saying, everything we say is strictly between you and me. I won't tell your parents, your teachers, anybody at all. That's a very important part of the relationship between doctor and patient."

"Who says I want to be your patient? I don't want a doctor. I'm fine. I don't see what all the fuss is about," Tom replied, crossing his arms tight across his chest. Dr. Brown nodded so slowly it looked as if he were in slow motion, and made general noises of agreement.

"I understand that, Tom. Look, I'm going to put my cards out on the table, as I feel it's crucial that we're honest with each other.

"Your parents are very worried about you. If they weren't, they wouldn't have gotten in contact with me. They know something is going on, they know you're talking to someone when you're alone in your room, they know that something upsetting happened at the castle, and all they are interested in is doing what's best for you.

"Which is where I come in."

He adjusted his tie yet again and smiled earnestly at Tom.

"I need you to prove to me, to convince me, that whatever's happening to you is real. Because if I can't prove to your parents that it is, then I can't help you. And if I can't help you, *then your parents might have to send you away to someone who can.*"

"Send me away?" asked Tom. "They can't do that, can they?" There was no concealing the worry in his voice.

"But let's hope it doesn't come to that," Dr. Brown said, brushing aside the question. He reached into his briefcase and produced a notepad and a pen. "So let's start at the beginning. Who is this person that your parents have heard you speaking to?" He tapped the paper with his pen, waiting.

Tom looked away, yawning loudly and pretending to be stretching, but secretly looking over nervously at Grey Arthur. Arthur shrugged. He could tell how worried Tom was. When he'd said, *"Send me away?"* it nearly made the room rock with that pang of fear, and now Tom was silently asking Grey Arthur what to do. It didn't feel like a particularly good situation to be in, whatever you did. Grey Arthur paused to think, weighing up the situation as best he could.

"If you have to tell him, then tell him. Do what you have to do to." He tried to look encouragingly at Tom, but he wasn't sure if he managed. Something didn't feel quite right about telling just a normal human all about the Ghost World, but Grey Arthur tucked these thoughts out of sight. He had to do what was best by Tom.

Tom nodded a thank-you at Grey Arthur, just a faint tip of the head, but Arthur noticed it and nodded back. Tom stopped his fake stretching and faced Dr. Brown. He took a deep breath.

"Okay, okay, I'll tell you what's going on. But I'm only doing this so you can go away and leave me alone. I don't need a doctor, and I don't want a doctor. I'm just doing this so you can convince my parents that I'm fine, that I don't need to go anywhere. Okay?"

Dr. Brown nodded.

"Okay," continued Tom, rubbing his forehead. He

really hoped this was the right thing to do. . . . "It all started a few weeks ago, when we moved down here to Thorbleton. I started at this new school, and I didn't have any friends at all, and some of the kids started picking on me . . ." Tom continued talking, picking up momentum as he got further into the story, and Dr. Brown began hastily scrawling notes.

Sometime Later . . .

"AND SO I LOOKED AT THIS SADNESS SUMMONER when I shouldn't have done, and I cried in front of everyone, which is completely embarrassing and I'll never live it down, and then to top it all off Mum and Dad must have heard me talking to Grey Arthur, which brings us to today, I suppose."

Grey Arthur had gotten bored a long time ago and was pacing around the room, trying to keep himself entertained. Dr. Brown dropped his pen and stretched his fingers, trying to shake off a cramp.

"And so that's it, pretty much," concluded Tom. He'd skipped some of the details, but the main bulk of the story was there. Bullied, car crash, Invisible Friend, castle, crying . . . He waited, nervously, to see what the doctor would say.

"Well. It makes for a very interesting story," said Dr. Brown, cracking his knuckles. "Sadness Summoners, Poltergeists, Chain Rattlers, Thespers, Faintly Reals . . . Hearing by emotion, being able to jump through walls, pick up objects. It's all *very* interesting . . ."

"But?" asked Tom. "There's a but, isn't there?"

"*But* . . . it doesn't prove anything. And if you want me to convince your parents, then I'm going to need proof."

"What kind of proof? I don't know what else I can do," Tom said sadly.

"Is he here? Is the ghost here?" asked Dr. Brown, glancing around the room.

Grey Arthur shook his head and waved his hands, but Tom ignored that.

"Of course he is."

Grey Arthur sighed.

"Okay." Dr. Brown reached down and picked up a toy car from the floor. "Do you mind if I use this?" he asked. Tom shook his head. "Okay, Tom. I need you to get Grey Arthur to move this car." He placed it on the desk before him and stared at it intently. "If I can see this car move without any apparent interference from either you or me, then that might go a way toward backing up your story. Because at the moment, that's

169

what it is. A nice story, an interesting one, but still just a story. So . . . let's get him to move this car."

"What if I don't want to?" asked Arthur.

"Arthur . . . ," Tom said under his breath.

"Okay, okay. But I'm only doing it because you want me to. Ghosts shouldn't do tricks. Dogs do tricks. And magicians. But not ghosts. So just this once, and just for you . . ." Grey Arthur leaned over and nudged the car with the tip of his finger. It moved a few centimeters before stopping after it ran into a sticky patch of spilled drink on the desk. It was, all in all, a distinctly underwhelming experience, but Dr. Brown reacted as if he'd just hit the jackpot.

"Did you see that?" he yelped, jumping up from the chair. "Did you *see* that car move?"

Tom shrugged. "Of course I did."

"Wow," said Dr. Brown. "Oh, wow. *Did you see that car move?*"

Tom didn't know what to say, especially since he'd just answered that question, so he just nodded quietly.

"So can you help me then? Convince my parents? Make sure I get to stay?" he asked hopefully.

Dr. Brown, eyes still wide, nodded enthusiastically, a huge grin on his face. Hurriedly he began throwing his notes back into his briefcase, hands clumsy in his haste.

"Of course, *of course* I can help you!" He grinned, flashing his off-white teeth. "This is just . . . this is

170

amazing. I'll be back tomorrow to do more tests, but definitely, I can help you. It'll take time, but we're in this together." He paused for a second, briefly tucking away the excitement, and put on a serious expression. He looked Tom directly in the eye.

"It is very important that everything we do and discuss here remains between us. No teachers, no school friends, not even your parents. If you were to talk about this, you'd undermine everything I'm trying to do to help you, do you understand? If you want this to work out, then you'll have to do as I ask." Dr. Brown nodded to himself, to some unspoken thoughts, and then smiled. "Yes. We must keep this a secret."

And with that, he left.

"Well, I thought that went quite well," said Tom. "Better than I was expecting, at any rate. Hopefully, with him on our side, we can get this all sorted out, and everyone will be happy."

Grey Arthur nodded politely but didn't say anything. He couldn't put his finger on it, but something just didn't feel right.

Real Life Beckons

TOM WENT BACK TO SCHOOL THE NEXT DAY. MUM had fussed even more than normal in the morning, straightening his tie at least three times before she let him out the door, making sure four times that he'd remembered to take his lunch, and insisting that he take a note with him with both her and Dad's work numbers on it. Just in case.

"Are you sure you're ready to go back?" she'd asked, and then, "You don't have to go back if you're not ready." Before finally, "And if you need us, don't hesitate to ring. Actually, would you prefer me to take the day off? Stay at home in case you want to come back?"

"I'm fine, Mum," Tom had protested as he edged toward the door. "It'll be okay. Honest. Stop fussing."

Dad had even offered to drop Tom at school, which was plainly ridiculous, because it only took about five minutes to walk there. Tom simply waved and dived out of the front door before his parents could attempt to wrap him in cotton wool or spit on a tissue and clean him.

The strange thing, though, was that nothing was directly mentioned about the castle, or Dr. Brown, or Grey Arthur. It was obviously the reason why his parents were acting so weird, but they never brought it up at all. Tom mused on that as he walked. Grey Arthur trotted alongside him, also lost in thought. Today was going to be hard work, going back and seeing the class after everything going so wrong at the castle, but Tom knew the longer he left it, the harder it would be. Still, knowing this didn't make it any easier. When he saw the school gates looming in front of him, his heart rate shot through the roof.

"Ready?" asked Arthur.

"Ready," replied Tom.

And in through the gates they marched.

The first lesson was with Mr. Hammond. All Mum and Dad's worrying had meant Tom was late for school, and he'd missed registration. Everyone was already sitting in class, writing. Tom stood outside the classroom, taking deep breaths, before pushing open the door.

"Sorry I'm late, sir," he said as he walked in. Grey Arthur followed, on his best behavior.

"Not at all, not at all, Tom. I wasn't even expecting to see you back so soon. Take a seat. We're just writing up our notes from the school trip."

Tom edged his way through the desks to get to his near the back of the classroom. As he walked past Big Ben's desk a foot shot out, and Tom stumbled. Big Ben laughed loudly.

"What's the matter? Are you going to cry again?

Marianne told me all about it," he said, jeering. Tom's face reddened.

"Get out," said Mr. Hammond flatly. "You heard me, Ben. Get out. Wait for me in the corridor. We don't need that kind of thing happening in here."

Big Ben growled and begrudgingly got up from his desk, all the while staring menacingly at Tom. Tom sank down into his chair and began unpacking his schoolbag, trying to avoid eye contact. Grey Arthur settled down beside him.

"It's not Ben's fault that Tom's a crybaby, sir," called out Kate.

"You too, Kate. Outside. I'll talk to you in a minute," Mr. Hammond ordered. Kate got up reluctantly and glared at Tom as she left the classroom, slamming the door shut behind her.

"Right, we'll have no more of that kind of behavior in my classroom. Do you understand?" said Mr. Hammond sternly. "The next person to say anything out of line can skip waiting outside the classroom and go straight to the headmaster's office, and explain to him why they're behaving so poorly. So does anyone else have anything to add? No? Good. Get on with your work."

A couple of other classmates gave Tom filthy looks after that, but nothing else was said. As Tom settled into his work, Mr. Hammond came over and crouched by his desk.

"I'm sorry about that, earlier. I'll have a word with them," he said in a hushed voice. "How are you feeling? Are you all right now? You didn't have to come back to school so soon, everyone would have understood if you'd needed a bit more time."

"It's okay, Mr. Hammond. I just want to get back to normal. I'm a lot better now," replied Tom, twirling his pen between his fingers awkwardly.

"Well, that's good. I'm glad you're feeling better. If you ever want to talk anything through, you know where to find me."

"Thanks," said Tom, "but I'm fine. I just want to get on with my work."

Mr. Hammond nodded and stood up. He nodded again and made his way out of the classroom into the corridor, gently closing the door behind him. Raised voices were heard, and after a while a red-faced Kate marched back in and sat down heavily at her desk. Big Ben didn't return. Mr. Hammond followed, and smiled reassuringly at Tom. The rest of the lesson passed in relative silence. It wasn't as bad as Tom had been expecting. Some kids even gave Tom sympathetic half-smiles when they caught his eye.

The bell rang, and as everyone surged out of the classroom, Kate sidled up beside Tom.

"I can't believe I got sent out of class because of you," she said, barging past, elbows out.

"That wasn't my fault. You didn't *have* to say

anything," Tom replied. Kate floundered at that, searching for a comeback. She hadn't been expecting Tom to reply.

"Whatever," she said finally, storming off. Whatever that meant. . . .

The rest of the day dawdled past. Sure, there was some whispering in the corridors, and some strange looks, and Tom was certain that he heard people mimicking his cry of "Ghost!" more than once, but it really wasn't as bad as it could have been. Pick-Nose Peter even approached Tom at lunchtime and asked if he really *had* seen a ghost. He didn't seem to be making a joke—he appeared genuinely interested. Of course, Tom said that Mr. Hammond had been right, and that it was most likely someone playing a prank on him, because Dr. Brown had made him promise to keep everything a secret, and perhaps it wasn't the best idea anyway to go revealing his ability to see ghosts to just anyone, but it felt nice to be talked to for once, instead of simply talked about.

Lunchtime, break time, home time came, and Tom found himself wandering home with Grey Arthur, strangely upbeat.

Dogs, and Magicians, and Ghosts

As promised, Dr. Brown turned up that afternoon. And the next. And the day after that. Over the weeks, the sessions with Dr. Brown continued, and with each passing session Grey Arthur was made to perform a new and more intricate task. He'd protest, complain, refuse, and sulk, but eventually he'd give in, because he'd see the look of worry on Tom's face.

"Please," Tom would whisper to Grey Arthur. "Please, if you don't do this, then Dr. Brown can't help, and if Dr. Brown can't help . . ." He wouldn't say any more, but then he didn't need to. Grey Arthur would sigh, and pout, but he would do as he was asked. It wasn't just magicians and dogs that do tricks, Grey Arthur did them too.

Pushing a toy car evolved into putting round pegs into round holes, and then into shuffling cards, and then into playing chess—something that Grey Arthur loathed, not least because he always lost. As each session progressed Tom became less and less involved, often just lying on his bed staring at the ceiling while Dr. Brown would excitedly arrange yet another new task for Grey Arthur. Grey Arthur would complain, Dr. Brown would clap his hands with glee at each new trick, and Tom would lie back on his bed, crammed full of secrets that he couldn't tell his parents. He consoled himself that this couldn't go on for much longer, and then soon he'd have a happy ending—his parents would no longer worry, Dr. Brown would need no further proof and would leave him alone, and Tom and Grey Arthur could go back to how it was before.

No such ending was forthcoming.

Instead the days just fell into a regular pattern—school, then home, then an afternoon session with Dr. Brown, then dinner.

Which was exactly how this day, two and a half weeks after first meeting Dr. Brown, was going. School, then home, and then . . .

Bingo!

DR. BROWN SHUT THE DOOR TO TOM'S ROOM AND, AS usual, wandered over to the desk, where he always sat. Tom sat cross-legged on the bed, and Grey Arthur was hiding underneath it. Today, instead of his usual brief-case, Dr. Brown carried a large plastic bag, and as he sat down he rummaged inside it.

"Something different for you today, Arthur," he

said, not even mentioning Tom. Tom was used to that by now. "Something just a little different . . ."

Dr. Brown took out today's test and proudly assembled it on the desk. It was some weird contraption, a sphere filled with numbered balls attached to a handle, and turning the handle caused everything to twist and turn inside the sphere before spitting out an individually numbered ball.

"This," said Dr. Brown dramatically, "is a bingo machine!"

Tom didn't look very impressed. "A what?"

"A bingo machine! Bingo! The game. Bingo?"

Tom looked blank.

"It's a game where you have to match the numbers up. Random numbers come out of this machine when you turn the handle." He illustrated this by twisting the handle round, and the machine spat out a little ball with the number "4" on it. "And you have to match those numbers up with the numbers you were given at the beginning of the game. First person to match all their numbers wins."

"Sounds like a dull game, if you ask me."

Dr. Brown ignored that comment and continued. "And so our task for today is to see if Grey Arthur can manipulate the way this machine works, to see if he can influence which numbers come through. Human hands can't reach inside the sphere and interfere, but ghost hands could pass through and, theoretically, pick and choose which numbers come through."

"Wouldn't that be cheating?" asked Tom. Dr. Brown ignored him.

"So will you ask him if he's ready to start the experiment?"

Tom heard a muffled, sulky voice from underneath the bed. "Tell him I can hear him, and I'm not coming out. I'm sick of doing these stupid tests. Tell him I'm on strike. What does it matter if I can affect bingo, anyway? Surely he's already got enough proof that I exist, and that you're not just making me up?"

Tom rubbed his forehead, chasing away the beginning of a headache.

"He wants to know," he said slowly to Dr. Brown, "why he needs to keep on doing tests. He says that surely by now you must believe he exists."

"Tom." Dr. Brown tugged on his beard. "Of course I believe he exists. I'm on your side, I really am. Your parents don't believe that Grey Arthur is real, and I am the only person who can convince them that he is. I'm not doing this for my benefit, I'm doing it for yours, and for theirs. I'm doing this to help you, Tom. And if Grey Arthur doesn't want to help you, then, well, there's nothing more I can do. . . ." Dr. Brown started to make gestures to pack away the bingo machine.

"Will you *please* do this, Arthur?" pleaded Tom,

hanging over the edge of the bed. Arthur sighed pointedly. "Please?" Begrudgingly Arthur crawled out from underneath the bed, but he didn't look happy about it at all. "He'll do it, he'll do it," said Tom anxiously. "Please don't pack it away." Dr. Brown nodded and left everything where it was.

"Is he ready?"

Grey Arthur sighed.

"He's ready," replied Tom.

"Brilliant!" Dr. Brown straightened his tie (which today was decorated with singing cats) and then began turning the handle. The machine whirred to life, noisily churning. "Okay, Arthur, it's very simple. The first number I want out is number eleven, so you must stop the other balls and make sure that number eleven is the one that falls out. On your mark . . . get set . . . go!"

And so it began. Hours passed, hours of calling out numbers, tumbling noises, handles being turned, hours spent with a very irritated ghost, an excitable doctor, and a very bored boy staring up at the ceiling.

"No, no, nine*teen*! Not nine!" Dr. Brown would cry, to which Grey Arthur would reply that Dr. Brown should stop complaining, that it wasn't easy, that it all moved around very fast, and that it was very complicated indeed passing his hand through one part of the machine while grabbing hold of something else. It was the ghost equivalent of patting your head and rubbing your stomach at the same time, growled Arthur. Of course, Dr. Brown heard none of this and would continue, oblivious. "No, no, no! Not forty-four! I asked for number six. Why are you giving me the wrong one?"

Tom just lay on the bed, studying the ceiling (there were three pieces of old tape left there from a poster that had long since been thrown away, one thumb-tack, and a spider spinning a web in the corner), and left them to get on with it. Over time, the complaints from Dr. Brown grew fewer and fewer, and it seemed Grey Arthur had mastered the art of picking out the right bingo balls.

"Next, twenty-six . . . twenty-six! Brilliant!" Dr. Brown clapped. "Fourteen . . . fourteen! Excellent! Excellent! Number two . . . two! Superb!"

And then Arthur refused to do any more. Random numbers spewed from the machine, and Grey Arthur sat cross-legged on the floor.

"That's it now, Tom. Tell him that's it. I've had enough. I've done more than enough to prove that I'm really here, and I'm not doing one little thing more."

"What's going on?" asked Dr. Brown. "Why have the numbers stopped coming out right? Is he still here?"

"Please," Tom said to Arthur, sitting up on the bed. "Please don't do this, Arthur."

"Do what? What's he doing?" asked Dr. Brown. He stopped turning the handle of the machine.

"I'm serious, Tom. I'm not doing one more thing. It's not right to keep making me do tricks. I've done more than enough by now," Grey Arthur said, crossing his arms.

Tom looked apologetically at Dr. Brown. "He says he won't do any more."

Dr. Brown's face darkened. "Did he now? Well, if that's the way he feels . . ." He packed away the machine, just scooping everything up and throwing it haphazardly back into the bag. He stood up and straightened out his tie. "I won't be here tomorrow, as I've got an important meeting to go to, so that leaves you a day to talk to your ghost friend, to talk him round. Do what you need to do. When I come back we'll see if Arthur is feeling a little more . . . *compliant.*" He paused, letting that sink in, before adding abruptly, "I hope, for your sake, he is." Dr. Brown marched out the door, shutting it behind him.

"Are you happy now?" snapped Tom.

"No, Tom. I'm really not," said Grey Arthur. He looked very serious. "Something doesn't feel right about all this."

"He's just trying to help me. If you were my friend you'd be doing the same." Tom turned over on his bed, looking at the wall.

"That's not fair, Tom," Arthur said.

183

"I'll tell you what's not fair. Having to be Freak Boy isn't fair. Being bullied isn't fair. Having to see stupid ghosts the whole time when I just want to be normal isn't fair."

"Tom—"

"I didn't ask you to be my Invisible Friend. I didn't ask to see ghosts. And, also, really, if you think about it, all this is your fault anyway."

"My fault? How is it my fault?" asked Arthur.

"Because if it weren't for you, then I wouldn't have remembered that permission slip and I wouldn't have been able to go to the castle and then I wouldn't have seen all those ghosts, and then Mum and Dad wouldn't have worried, and Dr. Brown wouldn't have to be here, that's how it's your fault."

"That's ridiculous! I'm just trying to do the right thing, that's all."

"And refusing to help Dr. Brown is the right thing?"

"Tom . . . something doesn't feel right about it all. Not all the tests, and certainly not the fact that he refuses to let you talk to your parents about it all."

"And you've suddenly come to this opinion? You were the one who encouraged me to talk to him in the first place."

"I know I did, and I thought it was the best thing to do, but . . . If everything about this doctor is okay, then why aren't you allowed to tell your parents?

What harm could it do? It doesn't feel right, having to keep it all secret."

"I had to keep you a secret. Besides, he's a doctor, he knows what he's doing."

"But why all the tests? One or two, maybe, but test after test after test? I just don't like it."

"It doesn't matter if you like it or not. Because of you, because of being friends with you, my parents might have to send me away to some specialist somewhere, and Dr. Brown is just trying to help me. If you were a good friend, you'd understand that."

"It's because I'm a good friend that I'm worried, Tom," cried Arthur, exasperated. Tom didn't respond, he just gave a long, exaggerated sigh, which annoyed Arthur even more. He moved to the far end of the room, arms still crossed, and that was where he stayed.

Very few words were shared between Tom and Arthur that night. A heavy silence hung between them, mouths clammed shut, each full of their own thoughts and concerns and not a small portion of grumpiness. Tom was convinced that Arthur was being deliberately awkward and unhelpful, and besides it was all his fault anyway; while Arthur was convinced that Dr. Brown just didn't "feel right" and Tom was being deliberately stupid not to realize it. They stood as far away from each other as physically possible while still being in the same room (which, admittedly, wasn't all that far apart at all, but when you're sulking, every little centimeter of sulking distance is incredibly important) and alternated between trying very hard to ignore each other and scowling at each other. When they did speak, the sentences were short and awkward.

"I'm going to sleep," said Tom.

"Me too," said Arthur.

"Good," replied Tom.

"I'm glad," said Arthur.

Tom jumped into bed, snuggling down underneath the covers in the grumpiest way he knew how, and Arthur crept beneath the bed, resting his frowning head on the Pretty-Betsy doll pillow.

"Arthur?" called Tom.

"Yes?"

"Good night, Arthur."

"Good night, Tom."

And out went the light.

Our Separate Ways

THE ALARM BEEPED TO LIFE, AND TOM GROGGILY reached out and turned it to snooze. Five minutes later, the alarm went off again, and Tom reached out and turned it off again.

Right on schedule, in came Mum.

"Come on, lazybones, out of bed." The curtains were pulled open, and outside the sky looked grey and bloated with rain clouds. Tom sighed. It was bad enough getting out of a nice warm bed on the best of days, let alone on a grey-skies-threatening-rain day, let alone on a grey-skies-threatening-rain *school* day. Tom tried out his best puppy eyes look on Mum, who wasn't having any of it. "Come on, out of bed. You don't want to be late."

Tom had yet to persuade his mum to let him lie in on a school day, to stay in bed and not go to any lessons, to just lounge around in his pajamas, read a book, eat ice cream in bed, maybe play some games. Of course, she let him stay home when he was sick, but what was the point of that? He was hardly well enough to enjoy it. Still, no harm in trying. Maybe one day she'd surprise him by letting him sleep in. Maybe. Tom doubted it.

"Now, don't forget that your dad and I are both working late after school tonight, so there are some leftovers for you in the fridge that you'll have to pop into the microwave. And just because nobody is going to be here, that doesn't mean you should be late home from school. We'll be back around five, shouldn't be any later than that, so you behave yourself—no wild parties while we're gone, okay?" She grinned at him.

"I'll be home on time, don't worry."

"I'll go and get breakfast ready. See you downstairs in a bit." Mum glanced around the room, and when Tom noticed she laughed nervously and shut the door after her as she left. Tom knew what she'd been looking for, though.

Mum and Dad never mentioned Grey Arthur or what was discussed with Dr. Brown. It was just a big hole in the middle of all conversations, and if the topic ever strayed too close, then everyone would just teeter off into awkward silence. Tom didn't know whether it was because Dr. Brown had told them not to mention it, or because they felt awkward talking about it, or because they just hoped that if they never mentioned Arthur, then perhaps Tom would just forget he ever existed. Sometimes Tom would catch Mum or Dad looking around the room, as if searching for someone, but as soon as they saw Tom looking they'd act ultra-normal—which didn't seem really all that normal at all. Dad would read the newspaper in an exaggeratedly normal way, and Mum would talk incessantly about normal things like the weather, or tea, or fish fingers for dinner, but she'd always talk a little too fast or animatedly. It felt like his ordinary human parents had been replaced by Faintly Reals, trying very hard to be just plain old nothing-strange-about-us human beings, but not quite getting it right. Still, his parents not talking about it made it easier to do as Dr. Brown asked and not bring up anything that was done in the sessions, so maybe Tom should be grateful for that. He leaned over the side of the bed and peered underneath.

"Wakey-wakey, Arthur."

Grey Arthur was still curled up beneath the bed. He opened one eye lazily and peered blearily at Tom.

"Come on, Arthur, time to get up."

"I'm not getting up." Grey Arthur yawned, repositioning the Pretty-Betsy doll beneath his head.

"Oh, come on, Arthur, you'll make me late for school."

"I don't think I'm coming in today, Tom. I'm having a day off from being an Invisible Friend."

"Are you still sulking because of Dr. Brown?" asked Tom. The blood was beginning to rush to his head, hanging over the edge of the bed like this. He could feel his cheeks and the tips of his ears getting redder.

"No, not at all. It's just I've got stuff to do."

"Stuff to do?"

"You know. *Ghost* stuff."

"Sure. Right." Tom sat up, leaving Arthur curled up beneath the bed. "Suit yourself."

Tom left Arthur shut in the bedroom and went downstairs for breakfast. Mum was doing some last-minute ironing in the corner, singing along to the radio. On average Mum would get pretty much every other lyric wrong, and she would always come in with the chorus too soon before stammering into silence and waiting for the song to catch up, but she seemed to enjoy the singing and that was the main thing. Dad was rushing around as usual, burning toast and struggling with a tie. Tom didn't understand why he didn't just get a Velcro one, since he seemed to wage war with his normal tie each morning, but apparently adults don't like making life easy for themselves.

"Mum told you that we're both going to be late home from work, didn't she?" asked Dad, as he managed to get his hand impossibly tangled in a knot of tie. A look of panic briefly fluttered across his face when he realized his fingers were trapped, but with an effort he managed to pull them free and began attacking the tie again.

"Yes, she did." Tom pushed his cereal half-heartedly around the bowl with his spoon. Breakfast didn't feel the same without having Arthur floating above his favorite chair.

"Good . . . And Dr. Brown can't make it over today because of a meeting, so you've got the afternoon to relax. Catch up on homework."

"Yes, Dad."

"And there are some leftovers in the fridge for you to microwave. But," Dad leaned in close and whispered conspiratorially, "if what she's left in the fridge looks scary to you, I've put some money in the drawer for you to grab some fish and chips."

"Cheers, Dad." Tom reached out and took over the taming of Dad's tie. In seconds he had managed to tie a perfect knot. Dad looked impressed, and then glanced at his watch.

"Well, you'd better get a move on. You don't want to be late for school."

You don't want to be late for school. Tom's parents would repeat this mantra every time Tom looked vaguely like he might be running late. The thing was, Tom really wouldn't mind being late for school. If he was really late, he might even miss the first few lessons. Incredibly late, and he might just turn up for lunch. Outrageously late, and he could just turn up at the school gates to hear the end-of-school bell, then wander back home again. Tom would very much like to be late for school, thank you very much.

Except, at the same time, Tom didn't want to be late either. Oh, yes, it starts off as just simple lateness, but then it all snowballs to surliness, rudeness, and the next thing you know Tom would be wearing all white, spitting all the time, and writing his name on walls or carving it into tables. Tom shuddered. Best to be on time, just in case.

Tom waved good-bye to his mum and dad, grabbed his schoolbag and packed lunch, and headed out the door. He glanced up to the top of the stairs before he left, to see if Arthur was there to wave good-bye, but the landing was empty. With a sigh he pulled the door shut and began the walk to school.

All by Myself

IT'S EASY TO GET USED TO PEOPLE, NO MATTER HOW outlandishly strange they are, and the walk to school felt empty without Grey Arthur trudging alongside Tom. The Snorgle living in the drain was in good form this morning, belching noises coupled with the occasional outburst of insults, but without Arthur to laugh and joke about it with, it didn't amuse Tom so much. He rummaged in his packed lunch and threw down the packet of cheese-and-onion crisps he had been given, and while the gasp of delight he heard made him briefly smile, it didn't last. Smiles last longer in company.

Agatha Tibbles was sitting on the crumbling wall outside Mrs. Scruffles's house, glaring at the passersby. Most of the children walking to school gave her a wide berth, which Agatha actively encouraged by hissing at people she didn't like, but when Tom approached she purred loudly and *mow*ed for attention. Tom dutifully obliged—after all, it didn't seem like a good idea to get on the wrong side of Agatha Tibbles. She nudged her head against him, covering his school uniform in different-colored cat hairs, but Tom knew better than to complain. Farther down the street, discreetly out of sight, he'd try to brush them off, but not here.

"I've got to go, you're going to make me late for school," he informed Agatha as she paraded up and down the wall, reveling in all the stroking.

Agatha *mow*ed.

"I know, I know, I'm sorry. Maybe me and Arthur will pop over one evening for tea, and I promise I'll make a fuss of you then."

Agatha Tibbles looked down the street, as if searching for someone. Tom sighed.

"Don't ask. He's at home. Sulking. It's a long story." Tom rubbed under the cat's chin and waved good-bye. "Say hello to Mrs. Scruffles for me." As Tom wandered off up the street, Agatha Tibbles watched him walk away, purring loudly to herself, before putting back on her Big Grumpy Cat expression to catch any stragglers running late for school.

It felt strange, walking through the school gates on his own. Everywhere he went, a constant nagging feeling followed Tom around, like the feeling when you've packed to go on holiday and know you've left something behind, but can't quite place what. Except this time Tom knew exactly what was missing. Or rather, who.

Maybe he shouldn't have been so hard on Grey Arthur.

"Oi! Freak Boy!" That old familiar call from behind him turned Tom's legs to jelly, and he kept on walking, refusing to turn round. *Big Ben. Pretend you haven't heard him, Tom. Just keep on walking.* "Don't you ignore me! *Freak boy!*" Tom picked up momentum, refusing to break into a trot but walking as fast as he possibly could without running. In his mind it was a lot better to walk away fast than run, because if you run they know you're scared and you look stupid, but Tom wasn't aware of just how silly speed-walking made him look anyway. His hips wobbled from side to side while he waddled forward. If Arthur was there, he probably would have pointed out that it looked ridiculous, but he wasn't, so Tom surged toward the school looking like a duck on a mission. His hands clutched tight around his schoolbag, and his heart raced. He pushed his way through the groups of children milling around outside, all standing there waiting for the bell to ring. "FREAK BOY, COME BACK HERE!" Almost in a panic now, Tom worked forward, heading toward the school entrance, people tutting and complaining loudly as he pushed his way through, but Tom had no time to care about that.

"FREEEEEAK BOY!" In his mind Tom pictured Big Ben chasing after him, pictured the rage on his face, pictured those big hands curling into fists. . . .

The school bell rang, and suddenly Tom was carried into the school in a wave of other pupils, lost from Big Ben's sight among the sheer mass of children heading toward registration. Tom nearly laughed with relief. That had been a close call. He'd grown a little too used to the Grey Arthur Inbound Bully Warning System, and that first shout had caught him completely off guard. Another thing to get used to without his ghost friend around.

The day dawdled on, dragging its feet. By break time it felt like it should be lunchtime. By lunchtime it felt like it should be home time, and by the time it was home time, Tom felt like he should be curled up in bed. It had been a long, lonely day. Ballpoint Bill had volunteered to keep Tom company during lunch, but quite honestly, it hadn't been the same. Bill, nice as he was, wasn't a great conversationalist, and Tom was convinced he finished lunch break with two pens fewer than he started with. Without Arthur's careful Invisible Friend duties, as well, Tom noticed that the notes had started up again. By midday he'd removed two from his back; one with the classic "Freak Boy" slogan and a new one that simply read "I cry at castles." He'd managed to avoid Big Ben for the rest of the day, but he still heard the other kids whispering behind his back. Sometimes people he'd never even met or seen before in school would deliberately barge into him in the corridor, and then walk off laughing together. If they didn't know him, how could they not like him? It's a strange world you live in when the ghosts make more sense than the humans, decided Tom.

The final bell was the best sound Tom thought he'd ever heard. He'd go home and apologize to Arthur, they'd make friends, and everything would go back to its own weird normality. It was a plan stunning in its simplicity and guaranteed to work.

He raced home, dodging the Spitting Kids, stopping quickly to pet Agatha, holding his nose as he ran past the Snorgle drain, running all the way (but taking extra care when crossing the road—you don't make that mistake twice!), running, running, down the alleyway, past the abandoned shopping trolley, into Aubergine Road, up to his house. He fumbled in his bag, finding the front door key, and unlocking the door he practically tumbled inside in his eagerness to make everything right.

"Arthur! Grey Arthur! I'm home!"

Silence.

"Arthur?" Tom kicked off his shoes in the hallway and raced upstairs, throwing open the door to his bedroom. "Arthur?"

Nothing.

He dropped to his knees, looking underneath the bed.

Nothing.

He opened the wardrobe, looking inside, just in case.

Nothing.

In desperation he searched the toilet, the garden shed, the kitchen, even under the kitchen sink.

Nothing.

Grey Arthur was gone.

Without a Trace

TOM SAT DOWN, PULLING OFF HIS SCHOOL TIE AND throwing it toward the laundry basket. The whole house was quiet: Usually Mum or Dad would be cooking dinner by now, the television would be chattering away to itself in the lounge, Cold Fish would be blaring out from the stereo in Tom's room, Grey Arthur would be talking or laughing or asking stupid questions, and the whole place would be flooded in a clash of different noises. Instead there was silence; horrible, heavy silence.

"Oh, come on, Arthur, where are you?" whispered Tom.

As if in answer, the doorbell rang. Tom leaped to his feet and rushed down the stairs, nearly tripping in his haste. Maybe Grey Arthur had locked himself out? No, no, that was stupid, ghosts didn't need keys. Maybe Grey Arthur was just messing about? Maybe he was practicing to be more human by ringing the doorbell. Maybe—

Tom swung open the door.

"Good afternoon, Tom," said Dr. Brown. Tom's excitement faded away. It wasn't Arthur after all. Dr. Brown was wearing his trademark chunky knitted sweater with the V-neck, and as he smiled he straightened his tie. Tom looked confused.

"You aren't supposed to be here."

"I know, I know, but the meeting was canceled. Something else came up. I hope it's not an inconvenience, but I've got something I have to show you." He hesitated, peering behind Tom. "Is Arthur with you?"

"No." Tom sniffed. "I think he's in a mood with me."

"Never mind, never mind. We can get him later. Come and have a look at this!" Dr. Brown began backing down the garden path, beckoning enthusiastically. "Well, come on, don't just stand there, Tom."

Tom peered at the garden path, and then down at his feet. He was wearing odd socks—one slightly grey and one bright white—and the path looked quite rocky.

"Hang on, just let me get my shoes on," he called after Dr. Brown.

"No, no. No need. Come out in your socks. This won't take two seconds. I've got something I have to show you in the back of the van."

"If you're sure . . . ," said Tom, hesitantly stepping out onto the path. The stones felt cold and rough beneath his feet.

"Definitely. Come on, don't dawdle. When you see this, everything will make perfect sense, you, the ghosts . . . Everything. Come on, *come on*."

Tom shuffled down the path, taking small steps. Dr. Brown gestured for him to hurry up and, grimacing, Tom trotted a little faster down the path until he was standing by Dr. Brown's white van. The doctor opened up the back door and pointed inside.

"It's in the back there. Go on, get in, have a look."

"It's in the back of the van?" asked Tom a little warily.

"What's the matter? Don't you trust me?" Dr. Brown looked questioningly at Tom, who didn't quite know how to respond. "Come on, Tom, we haven't got all day."

"Okay, okay, I'm going." Tom crawled into the back of the van. It was dark and smelled musty, like old rope, and old oil, and dirt. He had to crawl forward on his hands and knees, as there wasn't quite enough room to stand. "What am I looking for?"

"It's right at the back," came Dr. Brown's voice from outside.

Tom crawled farther in, struggling to see anything at all. "Are you sure, Dr. Brown? I can't see anything." There was no reply. "Dr. Brown?"

The van door slammed shut, plunging Tom into total darkness. Instinctively he crawled back the way he had come as fast as possible, hands clambering to find the lock in the poor light. When he finally did find the handle, the door was locked fast. "Dr. Brown! Let me out!" He worked hard to keep calm, but panic was beginning to creep in around the edges, and his heart pounded as he pulled and banged at the locked door.

The van engine roared to life, and a familiar lurching feeling and rumbling floor told Tom that they were moving. He huddled up in the corner of the van on the filthy floor, tucking his shoeless feet tight to him, hugging his knees to his chest.

"Where are you, Grey Arthur?" he whispered.

Reading Between the Lines

"THIS HAD BETTER BE IMPORTANT. I'M A VERY BUSY ghost."

Essay Dave reclined in his chair, his shiny shoes resting on his desk. The desk itself was covered in paperwork, paper clips, pens, staplers, pencil sharpeners, hole punchers, and every other item you could possibly ever hope to use in an office, and a few you most likely never would. All around the room, stacks of paper towered up toward the ceiling, each pile precariously balanced and in danger of falling at any second. The walls, the floor, the ceiling, the door, all lay hidden beneath a layer of notes, scraps of paper, and thumbtacks. An old fluorescent light, in its death throes, flickered overhead, and in the corner an electric fan whirred away, blowing paper across the room like pieces of tumbleweed in an old Western movie.

"It is," replied Grey Arthur, nodding sincerely. "Trust me."

Essay Dave swung his feet off the desk and stood up. He straightened out his suit (which was made entirely from old documents, contracts, homework, and reports carefully folded to make a sharp-looking outfit) and adjusted his tie. The words TOP SECRET ran down the length of the tie in big, red letters, and you just knew that someone, somewhere, was searching in a panic for that document, muttering the classic lines, "But I had it here a minute ago," "I don't know where it could have gone," and "Well, this is just ridiculous! Where could it be?" That's what Essay Dave did—he was the finest paperwork Poltergeist in the trade. If you've ever mislaid an important file just before a big meeting, or had your homework miraculously disappear from your bag, or written somebody's phone number on a scrap of paper only to have it vanish from your pocket/wallet/handbag/purse, then the odds are very high that you've bumped into Essay Dave. He never threw a thing away, and when you've been a Poltergeist for as long as Essay Dave, that meant an incredible amount of paperwork. The papers at the bottoms of the piles looked suspiciously like they'd been written with quills in Ye Olde English, while those nearest the top were all neatly printed on pristine white paper.

It was said that in his office, somewhere among these towering collections of haphazard filing, he had collected enough paperwork to know *something* about everyone.

Grey Arthur was hoping this was true.

"So, what was the name again?" asked Essay Dave.

"Brown," replied Arthur. "Dr. Brown."

Essay Dave strolled toward a pile in the corner of the room, sidestepping the other piles of paper. Grey Arthur followed him. Essay Dave hummed to himself as he perused the collection, thumbing through the different pages. Arthur was convinced this would cause the paper tower to collapse, and he instinctively took a step back, but somehow it managed to stay standing.

"Brown ... Brown ... Hmm ... Are you sure that's his name?" mused Essay Dave, as he searched through the papers. Grey Arthur shrugged.

"That's what he said his name was. Said he's ... Oh, what was it? An Eminent Expert in the Field of Child Psychology. Something like that."

"Hmm," said Essay Dave, stepping over to a different pile of paper. Kicking his feet slightly, like a swimmer does in water, he floated up to the highest sections, his head bobbing against the ceiling. He hummed louder now, his eyes scanning the stacks of paper, searching. Grey Arthur tried his hardest to wait patiently.

"You can come up if you like," offered Dave.

"No, it's okay," Arthur declined. Levitating slightly was one thing, but more than a meter and Grey Arthur tended to lose his balance and tilt over to one side, which was terribly embarrassing in the company of other ghosts. Especially one as famous as Essay Dave. "I'm more of a ground ghost."

"Of course you are." Essay Dave began taking articles off the top of the pile, examining them, and then throwing them to one side when he realized they weren't what he was looking for. The paper rather obediently floated down to the floor and formed a new pile in the corner.

"Aha!" cried Essay Dave, plucking a yellowing newspaper article out from near the top of the pile.

"Found you." He floated over to his desk and cleared a space by relocating all the junk to one side. Sinking back into his chair, he carefully unfolded the newspaper and gestured for Arthur to come over and have a look.

Grey Arthur didn't like what he saw.

LOCAL MAN IN FAKE DOC SHOCK
Reported by M. Shaw
Known criminal Gavin Snark was yesterday being hunted by police for allegedly impersonating a child psychologist.

Snark, age unknown, was practicing under the false name Dr. Brown, and claimed to specialize in child psychology.

Police were alerted after parents became suspicious of Snark's credentials. During an appointment with a young girl he forced her to perform a series of bizarre tests. It is alleged that Snark then threatened the child and became agitated, aggressively demanding that she "Prove that the ghosts are real!" Concerned by this behavior, the youngster's parents confronted Snark, who refused to answer any of their questions and fled the scene.

Snark, who is also wanted in connection with other crimes, including theft and assault, has not been seen since this incident. Police are advising parents to be on their guard and not to approach Gavin Snark if they see him, as he could be dangerous.

The article was dated from last summer and had been cut out of a local paper from an area Grey Arthur had never heard of. He picked up the paper and stared at it, not knowing what to say.

"Does that help you at all?" asked Essay Dave. Grey Arthur looked at him, eyes wide, mouth open. His natural grey color was fading to white. "Arthur?"

Clutching the newspaper, Arthur turned and ran. Straight through the office door, out into the street, running and running as fast as he could. Panic was gnawing inside him, and it pushed him faster, faster than he had ever run before. The wind howled in his ears, and colors blurred around him, and he pushed faster still, racing back to Aubergine Road. He ran so fast that his edges smudged even more than usual, and streaks of ghost streamed behind Arthur like the trails of a meteorite.

"Tom!" he yelled as he drew closer. "Tom!"

No matter how fast Grey Arthur ran, it wasn't fast enough. As he approached the house, he noticed with a jolt of fear that the front door had been left open. Tom's shoes were left just inside the front door.

Arthur raced upstairs, diving through the door to the bedroom. "Tom?"

Nothing. Tom's school tie lay on the floor near the laundry basket, and his bag had been unceremoniously dumped on the bed, but no sign of Tom himself.

Panicking, Arthur looked underneath the covers on the bed.

Nothing.

He popped his head into the wardrobe, looking inside, just in case.

Nothing.

In desperation he searched the toilet, the garden shed, the kitchen, even under the kitchen sink.

Nothing.

Tom Golden was gone.

A Long Way from Home

WHEN YOU'RE IN THE DARK, IT'S HARD TO TELL HOW much time has passed. The van rumbled down roads, turning corners, speeding up and slowing down, and Tom clung to the floor, his mind working overtime.

When the corners were taken too fast, he was thrown into the side of the van, and bruises started to collect on his arms. He banged on the walls of the van, begging to be let loose, banging until his fists felt near to bleeding, but it did no good. In the end he just gave up and sat in subdued silence, listening to the roar of the engine, the growl of spinning wheels, waiting. The ground underneath became rockier, and the van jolted around from side to side, making him feel queasy. After an age, the van slowed to a halt, and Tom tensed, waiting for what would happen next.

The van doors opened, and bright light flooded in. After the time spent in the darkness Tom had to squint, and he could see only the silhouette of Dr. Brown standing in the open doorway.

"What are you doing?" he yelped. Dr. Brown didn't reply. "Please, Dr. Brown, I don't understand why you are doing this."

"Tom," he said, very calmly. "If you cause a fuss, you'll only make things worse. Now come on, get out of the van."

Shakily, Tom crawled out of the van and got out, standing on unsteady feet, waiting for his eyes to adjust again to the light. They were in a clearing in the middle of a forest. A dirt track led away into the distance, crowded with tall trees. Mottled light worked its way through the leaves. Just beyond the clearing was a wooden hut. It looked abandoned, with grimy windows and an unkempt feel about it. Old leaves gathered around it, slowly turning to compost.

"Where are we?" Tom demanded.

"I thought we'd go to my house for a change," said Dr. Brown, leading Tom toward the hut. The doctor's voice lacked its usual warmth, as if he simply couldn't be bothered anymore. He reached out, and after some effort, pulled the door to the hut open and pushed Tom inside with an encouraging shove that caused him to tumble onto his knees. Shakily, he picked himself up again, brushing away the dirt with bruised hands.

The air in the hut was musty and stale, as if the windows hadn't been opened in a long, long time. The inside looked no better than the outside—books and newspapers were strewn across the floor, as well as food wrappers and remnants of old dinners. The space was divided into two, with a doorway separating the kitchen from the rest of the room. What Tom supposed was a bed, just a filthy blanket and a threadbare pillow, lay spread on the middle of the floor. Dr. Brown kicked it to one side, clearing space. A laundry basket in the far corner of the room was overflowing with dirty clothes, while a decrepit, dusty chest of drawers leaned against a wall, and flies swarmed around a bin.

"Don't worry about wiping your feet," joked Dr. Brown. Tom didn't feel much like laughing. "Take a seat." Dr. Brown grabbed a chair from the edge of the room, dragging it into the center, facing toward the kitchen. The legs of the chair scraped on the floor as it was pulled, making an unpleasant noise. Tom winced. Dr. Brown gestured for Tom to sit down.

"I don't want to," said Tom nervously.

"It wasn't a request."

Tom brushed crumbs off the wooden chair before sitting down on it. Dr. Brown walked behind him and took his hands, pulling them behind his back. Tom's heart raced, thumping crazily in his chest. He felt rope being tied around his wrists, being bound to the chair. Tom jerked his head to the side, voice rising in panic.

"What are you doing?" His voice sounded high pitched, which surprised him. "Is this some kind of test?" The rope was pulled tight around his hands—too tight—and Tom yelped.

Dr. Brown responded by tying a scarf around Tom's mouth, silencing him.

"Is this a test? No, Tom, this isn't a test. This is the actual thing." He took off his tie and pulled off that familiar brown chunky sweater, throwing them toward the already full laundry basket. They landed short and joined the clutter on the floor. He stretched. "You won't believe how good it feels to be rid of those disgusting ties," he said to Tom conversationally. "And that sweater itched like mad." He grinned, loosening the top button of his shirt to get more comfortable. "So . . . I expect you're wondering what's going on, yes?"

Tom nodded, eyes wide. Beneath the scarf his bottom lip was wobbling, and so he bit it to make it stop.

"*This* is what is happening." He reached into his trouser pocket and pulled out a ticket. "Do you know what this is? Yes? No?" Tom stared at him, blinking back tears. "Well, I'll humor you. It's a lottery ticket, more precisely a lottery ticket with my numbers for tonight's draw. My numbers, which, thanks to you, are going to win me several million pounds. My numbers, which your little ghost friend is going to ensure are chosen."

He crouched in front of Tom, at eye level, so close that Tom could smell the aniseed on his breath.

"I'm not really a doctor. You might have worked that out by now. I didn't even stay in school long enough to sit any exams. I've just been stumbling through life, the odd dodgy deal here and there, just enough to get by on, just enough to survive. And who wants to just survive?

"So I started thinking of the perfect crime, the perfect way to make money. And what could be more perfect than an accomplice that can walk through walls, an accomplice that's invisible? An accomplice that nobody believes even exists? Do you see where I'm going, Tom?"

Tom stared straight ahead, refusing to respond.

"Of course you do, you're a bright boy. So I started advertising myself as an expert, trying to find children who could see ghosts. An adult who can see ghosts is all very well, but you can't manipulate adults so easily. A child is ideal. So naive, so malleable . . . So I invented Dr. Brown. A novelty tie, an unfashionable sweater, a friendly smile—you'd be amazed what people will believe when they want to. Parents were queuing up to get me to see their precious child. Of course, as soon as I found out that the child couldn't really see ghosts I'd disappear, move on, on to the next child, on to the next set of worried parents. Again and again I'd be disappointed, and I'd move on. That is, until I met you, and Grey Arthur. See, until I met you, I was beginning to doubt ghosts really did exist, so I guess I owe you a big thank-you."

Tom wanted to scream.

"So here we are," continued Dr. Brown. "This is us. I finally meet a boy who can genuinely see ghosts, and suddenly my plan can work. Of course, there are a few tests along the way to make sure the ghost is up to the task, but you'll be pleased to know Grey Arthur passed them with flying colors. So you, and your ghost friend, are going to help make me a millionaire. And in return? In return I'll leave you alone, which might not sound like the best deal in the world, but let's face facts, you're hardly in the greatest position to negotiate."

Tom scowled at Dr. Brown, who just smiled back coldly.

"So, if I remember correctly from everything you told me, ghosts can hear by emotion, right? RIGHT?" Tom nodded hurriedly, and the smile disappeared from Dr. Brown's face. He grabbed hold of Tom's collar, twisting it so the fabric dug into his skin, and with the other hand he pulled the scarf away from Tom's mouth. "Are you scared?" he snarled.

"Yes," gasped Tom. "Yes!"

"Good. Then call him. NOW."

Rallying Cry

GREY ARTHUR WAS SITTING ON TOM'S BED, READING the newspaper article over and over again, searching for some hidden clue, some hint to where Tom could be. Worrying thoughts were churning round and round his head, making him giddy, when suddenly Tom's voice, familiar, loud, and saturated with fear, rumbled across the sky like thunder.

"GREY ARTHUR!"

Grey Arthur jumped to his feet, the newspaper fluttering from his hands to the floor. Tom's voice was calling out for him, and without a moment's hesitation

Arthur leaped out of the window, not even bothering to run down the stairs and out the front door, straight tumbling out of the double-glazed window and landing clumsily on the pavement. He picked himself up and immediately started running toward the sound of Tom's voice, toward the sound of his name being desperately called.

At the back of Arthur's mind he was thinking of how they had first met, with Arthur following Tom's shouting, except this time it was terror and not curiosity that spurred Arthur on, and he ran so fast that not even his thoughts could keep up.

Waiting

"He sh-should be on his way," stammered Tom, and Dr. Brown released the grip on Tom's collar. He nodded, pleased, and stood up.

"Good. You let me know the second he arrives." Dr. Brown wandered over to the doorway, disappearing briefly through before returning with an old, dusty television. He placed it on the old chest of drawers opposite Tom and plugged it in. The screen showed nothing more than hissing interference.

"Not to worry, we'll soon get a picture. It'll just take a while to tune in."

Tom just nodded dumbly. The man who had claimed to be Dr. Brown veered from intimidating to his old chatty self in the blink of an eye, and it made Tom feel very unsettled. An uneasy fear crawled in the pit of his stomach, and his shoulders and hands throbbed from the pain of being thrown around in the back of the van.

It was then that Grey Arthur threw himself through the shut door, tumbling to a halt just in front of where Tom was tied to a chair.

"Tom! What's going on? Are you all right? Why are you tied up? What's going on?"

"Dr. Brown isn't really a doctor," answered Tom, looking downcast.

"I know, I know all about it," Arthur said. Behind them, Dr. Brown turned round, leaving the television to buzz white noise.

"I take it that our ghost guest has arrived? I mean, I assume you're not talking to thin air?" Dr. Brown approached Tom, smiling disconcertingly. "Do you want to bring him up to speed?"

Arthur scowled at Dr. Brown. "What does he want, Tom? Are you sure you're okay? He hasn't hurt you?"

"You know the test he made you do yesterday

with the bingo? You have to do something similar, Arthur. But on a bigger scale." Tom's voice was shaky.

"How much bigger?" asked Arthur suspiciously.

"Bigger." Tom took a deep breath. "You need to fix the numbers for tonight's lottery."

"What's a lottery?" asked Grey Arthur, looking confused. Tom fumbled for an answer.

"It's a game adults play to win money. It's a bit like that bingo game you tried before, except you choose your own numbers, and if those numbers match the numbers that are drawn out you can win millions of pounds."

"And that's a lot of money?" asked Arthur.

"That's a lot of money." Tom nodded.

"And if I do this, he'll let you go?"

"That's what he says."

Dr. Brown watched this one-sided conversation with interest, smiling to himself. "I'll leave you two alone for a second to mull it over," he said. "I'll just be in the kitchen, so no funny business. You really don't want to get me angry right now." And with that, he walked through the doorway and out of sight.

"I could just untie you. Let you go," whispered Grey Arthur. Tom shook his head sadly.

"It won't make any difference. Even if I could get away, he'll tell Mum and Dad that I'm making this up, or that I'm crazy, and I can't run away from that. They trust him."

"Maybe we could prove it to them—I found this newspaper and . . ."

"It's no good, Arthur. Adults always believe other adults, that's the way it works. Who are they going to believe, Dr. Brown or a kid who they think is imagining ghosts? And anyway, he's not like he was, he's different. He's really scaring me, Arthur."

"So what do you want me to do? You want me to do this stupid lottery thing?"

"No," replied Tom, shaking his head.

"Then what?"

"I don't know!" Tom said. "I don't know what to do. There's got to be a different way . . ."

"I can't think of one," said Grey Arthur miserably.

Dr. Brown strolled back into the room, clutching a piece of paper.

"I think that's plenty of time. On this piece of paper I've written down the numbers that you have to choose for tonight's draw." He waved the piece of paper in the air in front of Tom. "So, what's it to be?"

Grey Arthur looked at Tom and smiled thinly.

He walked up to Dr. Brown and snatched the piece of paper out of his hand. Dr. Brown jumped, but then smiled gloatingly as the piece of paper vanished before his eyes, thrust into the invisible Grey Arthur's pocket.

"Good decision." He grinned coldly. "On the back

of the piece of paper is a map, leading to the television studio where the draw is being made. The show starts in less than an hour. We'll be watching the show on TV, so we'll know what's going on." He leaned in, placing a tight grip on Tom's shoulder, so tight it made Tom's arm twinge. "Tell your ghost friend that he'd better not let me down."

"He can hear you," snapped Tom.

"I know you don't want me to do this, Tom, but I can't see a choice," Grey Arthur muttered. "Once he gets this stupid money, he'll leave you alone."

Grey Arthur smiled reassuringly, and then turned and ran out through the wall. Tom watched him disappear from sight.

"Has he gone?" asked Dr. Brown.

"He's gone."

"Good." Dr. Brown reached over and pulled the scarf back over Tom's mouth. "Let's hope he doesn't let you down, for your sake." He turned toward the television and then hesitated, turning back to face Tom.

"Once this is all sorted out, who knows what else we can do together? We'll be unstoppable. Maybe we can even get the crown jewels. I've always fancied a shot at them." Dr. Brown winked, and Tom's heart sank. The light at the end of the tunnel snapped into darkness as a horrible realization crashed down on him. There would be no end, no freedom, no going back to normal after Grey Arthur had done this. With awful clarity, Tom saw a future of being forced to do whatever Dr. Brown demanded, of lying to his parents, of forcing Grey Arthur to be not an Invisible Friend, but instead an Invisible Thief.

If he had been able to talk, he'd have called Arthur back. He'd have shouted until his throat was raw, trying to undo it all, trying to find another way. But it was too late. Tom's mouth was gagged, and Grey Arthur was already on his way to the television studio.

An Empty Home

MUM INSTINCTIVELY KNEW SOMETHING WAS WRONG. The front door was wide open, and beyond the doorway a horrible stillness and silence clung to the house. There should have been noise, there should have been music playing, or the sounds of television, something, *anything*. There shouldn't be a wide-open door leading into a silent house.

"Tom?" Mum hurried through the front door, pulling it shut behind her. She dropped her handbag over the banister and noticed Tom's shoes kicked off by the front door.

"Tom?" Her keys, unused, remained clutched in her hand as she ran up the stairs. Unease prickled underneath her skin and made her heart beat faster.

"Tom?" His bedroom was empty. His schoolbag was abandoned on the bed, and on the floor lay his garish school tie. But still no Tom. Mum raced back downstairs, calling his name, louder this time.

"Tom!"

There was no response. Mum charged into the lounge, into the dining room, checking the backyard, searching the bathroom. Tom was nowhere to be seen, and the ugly gnawing feeling that something was wrong grew and grew until Mum felt giddy. She stood in the kitchen, hands pressed against the table, mind racing. Maybe she was overreacting? Maybe there was a rational explanation? Maybe she was being too protective? But still that feeling remained, the feeling that only parents really know, the worry that's bigger than words. Something wasn't right. . . .

The sound of the key turning in the front door lock snapped Mum out of her thoughts, and she dashed out into the hallway, expecting to see a grinning Tom appear, sheepishly explaining where he'd been. She'd already decided how she'd respond. She'd look stern at first, and lecture him for going out and leaving the door open, for not leaving a note, for not wearing shoes. She'd tut at the state he'd got his socks into, and then Tom would grin at her and apologize, and then she'd smile back because you can never stay angry with Tom for long, and then—

The door opened.

It was Dad, keys in one hand, briefcase in the other. He saw Mum's face, and his greeting smile dropped away instantly. "What is it?" he asked. "What's wrong?"

"Tom's not here."

"What do you mean, he's not here?" asked Dad, continuing before she could respond. "Well, he probably just got caught up after school."

"His shoes are here," pointed out Mum. Dad glanced down at the shoes left in the hallway and paused, thinking. "And his schoolbag and tie are upstairs in his room. But Tom's not here."

"Okay . . . Okay . . . ," he said, in his best calming voice. "He can't be that far away if his shoes are here."

"Something just feels wrong," said Mum slowly. Dad nodded, understanding.

"Maybe he's out with a friend?" he asked.

"Have you heard Tom mention any friends at this school? I haven't. Not one. And he'd leave a note. Tom would always leave a note. This isn't like him. Who could he be with?"

"Well, maybe Dr. Brown?"

"He's not coming today. He's at a meeting, remember?"

"Maybe he changed his plans. Perhaps they're out together?"

"Barefoot? He just turned up, unannounced, and whisked our son away *barefoot*?"

"Maybe. I don't know. Maybe it's some kind of bonding exercise?" Dad suggested weakly. Mum raised her eyebrows disbelievingly, and Dad shrugged. "At least phone him. See if he's with Tom, or if maybe he'd have an idea of where Tom could be. You're probably just getting worked up over nothing. You know how boys can be sometimes."

Dad picked up the phone in the hallway and handed it to Mum, who hastily began to dial Dr. Brown's number.

At the Other End of the Line

TOM STRUGGLED WITH THE KNOTS THAT TIED HIS hands but couldn't manage to get free. The rope itched and was knotted too tightly, and it felt like his fingers were beginning to turn red. He tried to get

Dr. Brown's attention, to get him to loosen the ropes, but the scarf tied around his mouth reduced everything he said to a muffled trail of vague noises. Even if he could get Dr. Brown's attention, he doubted very much he'd loosen the rope anyway. The kind, the compassionate, the sincere Dr. Brown had all been a disguise this man had worn to get what he wanted, and now that he no longer needed to play a role, all the smiles and kind understanding had fallen away. The person who was now there with Tom was cold, and dark, and looked as if he teetered on the brink of a terrible anger.

The new Dr. Brown was in the corner, still trying to adjust the picture on the television screen. Occasionally he would lose his temper and hit the screen before readjusting the aerial again. The sound of a television show sometimes surfaced from the noises of static, some cheerful man talking about the social lives of monkeys, only to be drowned out again in a sea of hissing interference a few seconds later.

"For crying out loud!" growled Dr. Brown, and he slapped the side of the television again. The picture flickered into clarity, and the sound cleared. "Finally!" He stepped backward slowly, wary of doing anything that could interfere with the reception. The picture remained. On the screen, a baby monkey clung to the belly of its mother, tiny hands clutching onto clumps of hair. The presenter spoke in a whisper, crouched behind a bush, careful not to disturb mother and baby. For a brief second Tom watched the telly, and he forgot where he was. He forgot the ropes, the scarf, the remote forest hut, the mission, the doctor who wasn't a doctor, and just for that brief second he listened to the whispered voice on the television, watched the mother monkey and the baby monkey, and everything else faded away.

The sound of Dr. Brown's phone dragged Tom out of his daydream and back into the room. The familiar sense of fear surged back, like that jolting sensation when a lift begins to move. Dr. Brown was rummaging in his pockets, trying to locate the source of the ringing. He found the phone in his back pocket and answered it, placing one finger across his lips as a warning to stay silent.

"Hello? Oh, hello, Mrs. Golden!" Tom's heart felt like it was stammering. His parents were on the phone. . . . "What's that? *Tom's gone missing?*" Dr. Brown gasped at Tom in mock horror before a wicked grin curled his lips. Tom could just about hear the faint tinny buzz of speech on the other end of the phone, but he couldn't make out the words. "No, I'm afraid I don't have the faintest idea where he could be, Mrs. Golden. . . . Of course, of course, I understand it must be *very* worrying for you. . . . Of course . . . Really, I'd help if I could, but I have no idea where Tom could be. . . ." He listened to the distant voice of

Tom's mum, nodding in silence as she spoke. Tom tried to call out, put everything he could muster into calling out to his mother, telling her he was here, telling her that Dr. Brown was nothing but a lie, a fraud, but through the scarf everything came out as a muted tangle of noise that stumbled short of being heard. Dr. Brown wagged his finger disapprovingly and walked farther away, beyond where the feeble sound would travel.

"Well, no, I wasn't scheduled to see Tom today anyway. . . . What meeting? Oh, oh, *that* meeting! Yes, I was supposed to be in a meeting right now, but would you believe, the stupidest thing happened? I was just getting ready to go when I somehow managed to trip over my own shoelaces and twist my ankle. Would you believe it? I know, I know, ridiculously bad luck . . ."

Out of the corner of his eye, Tom saw something move. An old, discarded newspaper rustled, just ever so slightly. Dr. Brown continued talking, not noticing, but as Tom stared the corner of the newspaper lifted up, and a little head with waving antennae peered out. It looked left, looked right, then looked left again before scuttling out from underneath the newspaper. *A Bug!* This bug stood up and gently brushed down her outfit. She was dressed as a fairly unremarkable beetle, her shiny domed back making her look perilously off balance, and an extra pair of arms flapped by her side, giving her four arms and two legs in total. She ran upright, like a person, and not like a beetle at all, which made her look faintly ridiculous, especially with her spare arms slapping from side to side as she picked up momentum. She ran across the floor, clutching a piece of paper in her tiny hand, and disappeared through a gap by the door. Tom quickly looked away, trying not to draw any attention. Dr. Brown continued talking, oblivious.

"Well, Tom is in a very fragile state emotionally right now. I hesitate to tell you, but he really hasn't been responding well to our sessions. . . . I really don't know what we can do, it all really depends on how *cooperative* Tom can be in the future." On saying "cooperative," Dr. Brown fixed his stare on Tom, and there was no escaping what was implied. Behave, Tom Golden. Do as I say, Tom Golden. *Or else,* Tom Golden.

"I'm sure Tom will turn up eventually, Mrs. Golden. After all, he's a good boy at heart and wouldn't want to cause you undue upset. . . . Okay, well good luck looking for him. Oh, Mrs. Golden? You will let me know if you hear anything, won't you? Thank you. Good-bye." He turned off the phone and smiled triumphantly at Tom.

"It seems your absence has been noted. If we get this done properly, we'll hopefully have you home by bedtime. But if you don't behave? Who knows. Children go missing all the time. . . . It's a dangerous world out there. You see it in the newspapers a lot, don't you? I mean, with all that stress you were under, children sometimes run away, don't they? Never seen again." He paused, as if mulling over the thought. Tom felt sick. As quickly as that, the dark expression left Dr. Brown's face, and he replaced it with a bland smile. "Now, I don't know about you, but I'm starving. Do you fancy a sandwich?"

Tom didn't respond.

"Well? What's the matter, cat caught your tongue?" asked Dr. Brown, but Tom just stared at him blankly. Dr. Brown rolled his eyes and approached Tom. "Do. You. Want. Some. Food?" he asked slowly, and pulled the scarf away from Tom's mouth.

"GREY ARTHUR, COME BACK! IT'S A TRICK! ARTH—" The scarf was quickly tugged back into place, smothering the rest of Tom's words, and Dr. Brown scowled.

"That wasn't very nice, was it?" he said darkly. He tightened the scarf around Tom's mouth, so tight it tugged the skin around his mouth painfully. "And there was me being kind and offering you some food. I won't make that mistake again. And I won't warn you twice."

Tom stared at Dr. Brown, all his hatred and betrayal and hurt carried with a simple look, and Dr. Brown just laughed. "Suit yourself. The bread's probably stale anyway." And with that he wandered into the kitchen, if such a dirty run-down room could be called a kitchen, whistling a happy song. He left Tom tied in the chair, and the television continued chattering away in the corner.

Meanwhile . . .

TOM'S MUM PUT DOWN THE PHONE, SHAKING HER head. Tears were beginning to gather in her eyes, making everything look slightly out of focus, but she managed to blink them away.

"Well?" asked Dad. "What did he say?"

"He hasn't seen Tom, and he's got no idea where he could be. The only reason he was even able to answer his phone was because he twisted his ankle and couldn't make it to his meeting."

"Okay," said Dad thoughtfully. He nodded, thinking to himself. A horrid fear began to grow inside him, but he tucked it out of sight, trying his hardest to look calm. "Okay, this is what we're going to do. Phone the school, and make sure that Tom went in today and that for some strange reason he isn't still there. Then, once you're sure he isn't there, *then* you call the police." He noticed the fear that flashed across Mum's face when he said that, and he quickly worked to reassure her. "Just as a precaution. I'm sure he's fine, I'm sure he is. But let's do this properly. Phone the police and let them know that our son's disappeared from home and that we're worried. They'll know what to do."

"And what are you going to do?" asked Mum.

"I'm going to go out and look for him. You stay here in case he phones or comes back, and I'll have a quick look around the neighborhood." He leaned across and kissed her good-bye. "He'll be fine. I'm sure he will."

Dad hoped that he sounded convincing. He certainly didn't feel it.

Mum smiled thinly back, but all the while the sensation of something being wrong still clung to her and made her feel cold through and through. Dad left, shutting the door behind him, and Mum began to shakily dial the number for the school. . . .

And Elsewhere . . .

IF GREY ARTHUR HAD THOUGHT THAT SCHOOLS WERE loud, then television studios were deafening. The walls hummed, the air shook, and the ground trembled with the accumulated wishes and dreams of people; fingers crossed, lucky socks, and high hopes. The mutters became a clash of sound, individual voices impossible to pick out as everything merged into a solid wall of emotional noise:

> ". . . IMAGINE WHAT I COULD DO WITH THAT MONEY. . . . I WISH IT WAS ME, I WISH IT WAS ME. . . . I'M GOING TO BE ON TELEVISION! I HOPE MY HAIR LOOKS OKAY! I REALLY NEED THIS MONEY, MY LIFE WOULD CHANGE IF I WON THIS MONEY. . . . PLEASE, PLEASE, PLEASE, PLEASE, PLEASE . . . MY STAR SIGNS SAID TODAY WOULD BE MY LUCKY DAY! FIRST THING I WOULD BUY IS . . ."

And on and on the voices went, sounds crashing down on poor Grey Arthur until he wanted to curl up in a ball and scream for it all to stop.

But he didn't. He couldn't. Tom was depending on him.

Grey Arthur stepped up onto the stage and sat down cross-legged on the floor (or more precisely, floating about two centimeters above it) and waited for the machine to be wheeled onstage, for the cameras to start filming, and for the show to start.

"I won't let you down, Tom," said Grey Arthur, and he couldn't even hear his own voice above the shouting of all the hopeful humans. "I promise."

And Tom's voice, calling out, filled as it was with fear and anger and hurt and concern, calling out for Arthur to come back, that it was all a trick, went unheard, lost in a sea of other shouted hopes.

News Flash

"WHAT ARE WE DOING HERE?" MIRANDA PUSHED A particularly foul-smelling sock out of the way and peered into the room. The place looked practically abandoned, and smelled like a herd of Snorgles had had a wild party in there the night before. "Are you sure this is the right place?"

"Of course I am," replied Mike, hauling himself out of the laundry basket beside her. He grabbed a sock out of habit and shoved it into his pocket. "The *Daily Tell-Tale* said there was a job here. Should be a piece of cake, it's only a simple shoelace tangling, and then we can be gone."

"Shoelace tangling? That's so amateur." Miranda sniffed snootily. "Next time I choose the job."

"It's all good Poltergeisting experience. I don't know why you're complaining. It's been a while since we did a decent shoelace tangle anyway. Mind you, the last one was a toughie. You remember? The guy who lied about tripping over his laces, but was actually wearing slip-on shoes? That was a challenge! I thought we handled that very well, especially when you—"

"Shush!" hissed Miranda.

"Shush?" Mike whacked her playfully round the head with an abandoned sock. It felt distinctly crispy. "Why are you shushing me?"

"SHUSH!" she growled. "Over there . . . in the chair."

Mike looked over at where Miranda was pointing. Sure enough, in a chair was a human boy, hands tied together. His back was to them.

"Isn't he the one who can see ghosts?" whispered Miranda.

"Don't be daft." Mike laughed.

"No, I reckon he is."

"Humans can't see ghosts. Someone's pulling your leg."

"No, it's true," replied Miranda, insistent. "He's Grey Arthur's pet human, and he can see ghosts. A Thesper told me. I'm pretty sure it was in the paper too!"

"How can you tell it's him? You can only see the back of him, and you know how all humans look the same. Besides, you should know better than to believe a Thesper."

"If you don't believe me, go and stand in front of him and have a look."

"That's stupid. Anyway, we came here to do a job, not play with a silly human."

"You're scared," said Miranda.

"I am not," Mike answered. "I just don't see the point."

"*I dare you,*" said Miranda, grinning widely. Mike sighed. You can beg, demand, coerce, cajole, insist, or plead with a Poltergeist to do something, and chances are that it will refuse, just to be annoying, but no Poltergeist can ever resist the overwhelming pull of a dare.

"Fine!" Mike stood up and marched in front of the boy in the chair. He leaned forward, and poked out his tongue at him. "See?" he shouted at Miranda, before peering closely at the human boy's face. "Nothing." The boy locked eyes with Mike and let out a muffled cry. Mike screamed and dashed back over to Miranda, practically crashing through the wall in his haste.

"He can see me!" he squeaked, leaping behind a pile of dirty clothes.

"I told you so! He's Tom, Grey Arthur's pet human. What did he say?"

"I don't know, he's got a scarf tied round his mouth."

"Why's he got a scarf tied round his mouth?" asked Miranda.

"I don't know. Maybe his mouth was cold. Humans are weird."

Tom gave out another muffled noise, which made Mike and Miranda jump.

"Maybe it's a game?" suggested Miranda, nudging Mike back toward Tom. "Ask him if it's a game."

"You ask him!" Mike said, refusing point-blank to move. "I don't want to go near him. He's creepy. It's the way the eyes follow you around the room." He shuddered at the thought of it.

"You're such a chicken." Miranda sighed, shaking her head.

"Well then, you do it. *I dare you.*"

"Fine, I will," she replied. She didn't move.

"Well, go on then."

"I'm just . . . getting ready."

"Chicken."

Miranda glared at Mike and began taking timid

steps over to Tom. Slowly, she edged around so she was facing him, and gingerly she reached out and tugged the scarf down from around his mouth. Immediately she leaped back a step.

Tom took two shuddery breaths, and his chin began to wobble, and he crumbled into tears.

"You've broken him!" yelled Mike, from his sanctuary behind the pile of dirty clothing. "What did you do?"

"I don't know! I didn't mean to break him!"

"Well, undo it! Make it stop! He's hurting my ears!"

"I don't know how!" Miranda was rooted to the spot, unsure of what to do. To an average human, the noise Tom was making would have been barely louder than sobs, but to the ghost ear, geared toward hearing emotions, it was as deafening as a marching band. "Do you think that's why the scarf was there in the first place? To stop him from making this awful noise?"

"Well, put it back then! Make it stop!" shouted Mike, and Miranda reached a shaking hand out to pull the scarf back into place. Tom shook his head desperately.

He finally managed to find some words, squeezing them in between gaps in his sobs. "I've . . . been . . . kid . . . napped," he cried, struggling to get his tears under control. He sniffed, held his breath, concentrated, and made a concerted effort to stop his sobbing. "I've been kidnapped," he repeated, his voice squeaky from the effort of holding the crying at bay. "And he's using me to get Grey Arthur to rig the lottery, because then he said he'd let me go, but he won't let me go, not properly, he'll just keep on using me and Grey Arthur forever and ever, and so I have to warn Grey Arthur but I don't think he can hear me because I shouted and he hasn't come back and . . ." Tom looked over at the kitchen and saw Dr. Brown making his way back over. "Put the scarf back! He's coming, put it back over my mouth!"

A rather bemused Miranda reached over and pulled the scarf back over Tom's face.

"Do you think humans always talk this quickly?" she asked Mike.

"Do you think they always make so little sense?" Mike asked Miranda.

Dr. Brown waltzed back into the room, eating a sandwich made from bread that was so old it curled in one corner and had blue patches on the crusts.

"You been behaving yourself, Tom?" he asked, taking a bite. He chewed noisily. Tom nodded. "Aww, have you been crying? What a little crybaby." He laughed and turned to walk away. Or at least that had been the plan. Somehow, his shoelaces had become hopelessly tangled together, and he tripped, landing in an undignified heap of legs and elbows on the floor. A strange noise escaped him, part yelp, part shout, part scream, part holler, which trailed into a whimper. He sucked in air through gritted teeth and wrapped his hands around his foot, rocking slightly.

"My ankle!" he screeched.

If he could have seen beneath the scarf that was wrapped around Tom's mouth, he would have seen the flutter of a smile that was soon drowned in worried feelings. If the scarf hadn't been there, Tom would have muttered a thank-you to the two ghosts that had just crawled away through the laundry basket, and a prayer that they would get help. Instead Tom simply sat in silence, hoping a hidden hope that the strange ghosts that had appeared in the hut knew how to reach Grey Arthur, knew that Tom was serious, and knew how to make everything right.

It was a lot to wish for, and that made Tom's hope a little fainter, and seeing the anger on Dr. Brown's face made it nearly vanish altogether.

Dr. Brown staggered to his feet, wincing, and limped over to a chair. He dragged it across the room and positioned it next to Tom's, facing the television.

"Talk about bad luck," he growled, settling into the chair. "I mean, what are the odds?" He cradled his ankle in his hands, trying to rub away the pain. He glanced at his watch and then grinned a yellow-toothed grin at Tom, the pain momentarily forgotten. "Not long now, eh? Let's hope your ghost friend gets this right, or there'll be hell to pay."

He got out his ticket and a pen from his pocket,

ready to tick off each number as it came through, and stared expectantly up at the television. Not long now at all.

The next few minutes dragged and dragged. Longer than a lonely lunchtime, longer than a double maths lesson, longer than a day at school without a friend. Slow minutes dawdled past, and the two sat side by side—Tom tied in his chair, mouth bound, Dr. Brown slumped in his chair, ankle swelling, one hand clutching a lottery ticket, the other hand clutching a pen. Tom glanced around nervously, waiting, hoping, expecting help at any second.

Waiting.

Hoping.

Not long now.

The theme tune for the lottery began and Tom's heart sank. It was too late. No rescue, no plan, no hope. Dr. Brown was going to become one of the richest people in the country, thanks to him, and that was just going to be the beginning. . . .

"Hello, and welcome to tonight's lottery draw!" chirped the incessantly happy woman on the television.

Dr. Brown grinned ecstatically and nudged Tom. "Here we go!" he cried. Tom shut his eyes. He couldn't even bear to look.

The presenter—perfect smile, flawless skin, hair hairsprayed solid—continued on the television screen. "Tonight's total prize . . . Tonight's total . . ." She faltered, her perfect smile dropping slightly, then she shook her head and continued. "Tonight's total prize . . ."

And suddenly, just like that, on live television, she burst into floods of tears.

Smile for the Cameras

"OH MISERY, MISERY!
Thought of beneath the willow tree!
My heart, full of sorrow, full to bursting,
Is it my tears for which you're thirsting?
Oh such sweet, sad, forlorn poetry!
Thought of beneath the willow tree!"

Woeful William glanced over at Mrs. Scruffles, who smiled encouragingly and signaled for him to continue. Holding a scroll of paper at arm's length, he nodded and read on, gesturing emphatically with his spare hand, which was clutching a frilly handkerchief.

The television presenter, who was standing next to Woeful William, faltered.

"Tonight's total prize . . . Tonight's total . . ." She

paused and shook her head before trying to continue again.

"Stand closer to her!" hissed Mrs. Scruffles, and Woeful William took a few steps nearer until he was talking directly into her ear (for which he had to stoop slightly, being of a lanky build). He flapped his handkerchief in front of her face dramatically.

> "Alas, Alack, Tragedy, Woe!
> Chin-wobbling tears are wanting to flow!
> My sweet, my dear, do not defy
> That overwhelming urge to cry!"

"Tonight's total prize . . . ," she said, and then burst into floods of tears. The cameramen looked at each other, unsure of how to react, and the audience gasped. The presenter stood there, huge wracking sobs taking over her, fat tears falling from her eyes and dragging her mascara down her face. Her nose began to drip as well, and she sniffed noisily in between sobs. Worried glances were exchanged between the back-stage staff, and the audience sat in awkward silence.

"I thank you!" declared Woeful William, bowing deeply with a flourish. "I thank you!"

Mrs. Scruffles clapped.

A very nervous-looking Grey Arthur looked on.

"I don't get it. What now?" asked Arthur, twisting his fingers anxiously. "I'm supposed to be fixing the numbers, not making some woman cry. And why are you here anyway? How did you know?"

The presenter ran past the ghosts, still sobbing manically, chased by a nervous-looking producer.

Mrs. Scruffles replied, "The Mischief Twins bumped into your friend in Duskridge Woods, and then they came straight round to visit me. Apparently young Tom is in quite a pickle. You should have told us in the first place, Arthur, instead of doing what that ghastly man demanded."

"I just wanted to fix everything so Tom would be okay." Arthur sighed. "And I still don't see how a crying woman is any help at all."

"Well, my dear ghostly companion," replied Woeful William, "what we are doing is buying some time." He pushed his handkerchief back inside his sleeve and threw the poem into the air, where it promptly disappeared. "The real plan is just beginning."

"Which is?" asked Arthur.

As the chaos continued around them, the cameramen standing around shrugging at each other, the television presenter still sobbing her heart out in a corner, the producer running around wild-eyed not knowing what to do, Mrs. Scruffles smiled warmly and carefully explained it all, as Grey Arthur listened intently.

Normal Service Will Resume

"WHAT ON EARTH IS *WRONG* WITH THAT STUPID woman?" screeched Dr. Brown at the television. Tom gingerly opened one eye and looked at the screen, just in time to see the presenter crumble into hysterical tears. "Talk about unprofessional. Get on with it! It's just not my lucky day today. Come on, sort it out!"

As the camera panned out, Tom sat bolt upright. There onstage next to the weeping presenter were Grey Arthur, and Mrs. Scruffles, and a ghost that looked like it had to be Woeful William. Tom realized he was staring excitedly, and he tried his best to look miserable. Grey Arthur stepped in front of the camera and delivered a speech that had an intended audience of one—a normal human viewer would be oblivious, but Tom saw him and had to suppress the urge to laugh with joy. Grey Arthur spoke to the wrong camera, and so was staring off to the left instead of straight ahead, but considering that it was his first time on live television he did remarkably well.

"Hold tight, Tom. Help is on its way," was all he managed to say before the screen went blank. It was replaced with a notice apologizing for "technical problems." "Normal service will resume soon," it said.

"This is plain ridiculous. Today of all days," growled Dr. Brown. He was clutching his ticket, all ready to tick off the winning numbers. "I hope they get this sorted out soon."

It was then that Dr. Brown realized his pen was missing.

"What? Where's it gone? It was here a second ago, right here, on the arm of the chair. Where the blazes has that pen gone? It can't just disappear! Pens don't just disappear!" He stood up, limping across the room, searching for the elusive pen. He lifted up newspapers, looked under books, muttering foully under his breath.

"You haven't seen my pen, have you?" he barked at Tom, who shook his head, looking the picture of innocence. "I need that pen! You'd better not have taken that pen, Tom. I'm not in the mood for stupid games. I need that pen! How else am I going to mark off my numbers?"

Ballpoint Bill waved at Tom, smiling reassuringly as he chewed the tip of Dr. Brown's precious pen. Completely unaware, Dr. Brown limped past him, scowling.

"It has to be here! Where the hell is it?"

Ballpoint Bill nodded to Tom, placing a finger over his lips to tell him to be quiet, and disappeared back into the laundry basket he had crawled out of just moments earlier.

There was a knock at the door, and Dr. Brown looked at Tom in horror.

"Not. A. Word. Do you understand me? If you so much as make that chair creak, so help me . . ." He limped over to the door and opened it a crack. "What do you want?" he snarled through the door.

"Now, that's not a very polite way to answer the door," said the voice on the other side. Her voice sounded friendly, and warm, and very familiar.

"I'm busy," replied Dr. Brown, trying to get rid of her.

"This won't take long," she said calmly.

"It better not. I don't want to miss the lottery."

"My cat is stuck up a tree. Would you be able to help him down?"

Which was when Tom worked out who it was at the door. It felt like a weight had been lifted from his chest, and he could finally breathe again.

"No! Just . . . go away!" Dr. Brown slammed the door shut, and the woman began persistently knocking at the door again. He tried ignoring it, but she wouldn't stop. He glared at Tom.

"I'm going to have to get rid of this daft bag. I'll be two minutes. *Two minutes*. So don't get any clever ideas. I'll be back before they start the actual draw." He glanced at the television, which was still promising that normal service would resume shortly, and sighed deeply. "All right, all right, lady, I'm coming. Stop banging on the door." He opened the door a crack and slipped out of the hut.

Cat Rescue

"WHAT ON EARTH ARE YOU OR YOUR CAT DOING ALL this way out here in the woods anyway?" grumbled Dr. Brown, as the woman led him toward a particularly tall tree.

"I was just taking him for a walk," said the woman sweetly.

"You take your cat for a walk?"

"Doesn't everyone?"

Dr. Brown rolled his eyes. "If you say so. Let's just get this over and done with," he said.

They stopped by a tall tree. Chestnuts were scattered all around its roots, spiky casings burst open. A scrawny ginger cat was clinging to one of the branches, howling dramatically. He was quite possibly the most pathetic excuse for a cat that Dr. Brown had ever seen—tangled, knotted hair and a feeble-looking tail, and a meow that sounded ridiculously high-pitched.

"If you could just get him down, that would be ever so good of you," said the lady.

"You want me to climb the tree?"

"Unless you have a ladder?"

"Look, lady, I'm not in the business of climbing trees to rescue mangy-looking cats. I've got a TV program I need to watch. I don't have time for this." Dr. Brown turned to leave.

"That's fair enough. I'll just call the fire brigade and get them to come out here. Maybe I could wait in your hut until they arrive?"

Dr. Brown sighed and rolled up his shirtsleeves. The last thing he needed right now was more people turning up in the woods. "Fine. I'll do it. Just . . . Just wait here. Don't go wandering off." He began climbing the tree—not the easiest thing with a swollen ankle—and made slow progress up the branches.

"Thank you so much for doing this!" called the woman from the ground. "You really are a gentleman!"

Dr. Brown growled, and climbed higher. Anything to get rid of this deranged woman and get back to the television. The ginger cat meowed at Dr. Brown and leaped to a higher branch, and it was all Dr. Brown could do to stop himself from screaming with rage.

"You're ever so good for helping us!" called the woman from the ground. "Ever so good!"

The Legend Himself

BEHIND HIM TOM HEARD A GROANING NOISE AND THE sound of things being pushed aside. He tried to turn his head, but he couldn't turn it far enough to see what was going on.

"It's been a long time since I've had to do that!" roared a voice from behind Tom. "Are they making laundry baskets smaller these days? I certainly don't remember them being such a tight fit!"

A ghost marched in front of Tom, grinning widely. This ghost that towered in front of him was larger than life and twice as loud. His clothes were all in deep shades of red, from the huge scarf that was wrapped round his neck down to the worn old leather boots, tied with pieces of red string. He had a big, bushy beard and a mustache that twisted off into little points. His voice boomed, rich theatrical tones like the rumble of distant thunder.

"Now, you must be Tom," he bellowed.

Tom knew who this had to be. Grey Arthur's hero, the master of the Elephant's Exodus, mastermind of the disappearing building. The Poltergeist all other Poltergeists aspire to. He leaned over and pulled the scarf away from Tom's mouth.

"Red Rascal!" breathed Tom. The Red Rascal laughed, a hearty uproar that sounded very much like the noise an amused lion would make.

"At your service!" He bowed with a flourish. "I hear you're having a spot of trouble with a human. Not to worry. Everything is being taken care of." He snapped his fingers and the ropes that had tied Tom to the chair simply fell away to the ground. Tom shook his hands and tried to massage some feeling back into them. They were still shaking.

"Where's Grey Arthur? Is he coming back?" he asked.

"Don't worry yourself, Tom. He'll be with you soon enough, he just had something he needed to do first."

"What about my parents? They know I'm missing—they'll be worried sick. We have to let them know I'm okay."

"Never fear, young Tom, it's all being taken care of."

"And what about Dr. Brown? He'll be back any second. He just popped outside. Then what?"

"Then," the Red Rascal said, grinning, "he'll see that the hut is missing." He saw the confusion on Tom's face and laughed. "I didn't get my reputation for nothing, you know!"

Tom leaped from his chair and dashed over to the nearest window. He spat on his sleeve and used it to clear a spot in all the grime that clung to the glass.

The hut was in front of a row of trees, and at first Tom thought that they were still in the woods. However, when he looked harder, he realized that beyond the trees was something that most definitely wasn't those woods: a perfectly manicured lawn, stripes of lighter and darker green stretching out and out for acres. Nearby, an extravagant-looking stone fountain, stacked high with angels and lions and cheeky cherubs, cascaded with crystal clear water. Rows of perfect-looking flowers framed the scene.

"Where am I?" asked Tom, face pressed to the glass. His breath steamed up the window, and he quickly used his sleeve to wipe it clean.

"Somewhere safe. In fact, the safest place in the whole of England."

"You've stolen the hut and moved it?" asked Tom incredulously.

"Borrowed it. Temporarily." The Red Rascal nodded. "Trust me, the woods are no place to be a human right now. . . ."

A Treetop View

"COME ON, GET OUT OF THE TREE, YOU MANGY CAT! I've only got a few minutes until the draw is meant to be done!" hissed Dr. Brown, clinging on to the branch with one hand and stretching out toward the cat with the other. The cat hissed back and retreated farther into the tree. Dr. Brown edged forward, legs wrapped around the branch, but every time he moved the ginger cat anticipated it and shrank just out of reach. "It's no use, lady. This cat's not coming down, and quite frankly I've got better things to do with my time." There was no response. Gripping tightly, he peered down to the ground. "Lady?"

There was nobody there. "Oi!" he called out. "Don't just get me to climb a tree and then wander off. Where've you gone? For crying out loud . . ."

On the ground below, a large Persian cat emerged from the bushes. She looked up at the tree, and *mow*ed. The ginger cat Dr. Brown had been struggling to reach meowed loudly back and leaped gracefully down from the tree. Dr. Brown spluttered with rage.

"What? You could get down on your own this whole time?" he growled, clambering down the tree. He dropped down from the lowest branch, landing awkwardly on his sore ankle. "Come here, you flea-bitten furball! I'll teach you a lesson about wasting people's time! And where's your owner gone? Crazy cat woman. She'd better hope I don't catch up with her as well." As Dr. Brown stalked after the cat, limping and cursing all at once, it struck him that something was missing.

Something very important.

"MY HUT!" screamed Dr. Brown. "SOME-ONE'S TAKEN MY HUT!"

The ginger cat meowed, a shuddery sound that—if cats could laugh—would sound very much like a cat laughing. Dr. Brown lunged, but both the cats were too fast for him, scattering in opposite directions, disappearing from sight, swallowed up by the greenery of the woods.

"What is going on?" roared Dr. Brown at the empty woods. "Tom! TOM! If this is your idea of a joke, you won't be laughing when I get my hands on you! *TOM!*" His own voice echoed back at him, tauntingly shouting Tom's name. Dr. Brown leaned against a tree, hands curled into fists. Where the hut had been, all that remained was a large rectangular patch of dirt. Earthworms sprawled on the surface, trying to burrow their way back into the ground. "I bet you think this is pretty clever, don't you?" screamed Dr. Brown into the air.

As if in response, the early evening sun disappeared behind a cloud and a darkness descended on the forest. With the light no longer dappling through the leaves above, the autumn heat drained from the woods, and cold began to cling to Dr. Brown's skin. He shivered, rubbing his hands against his arms, and began to regret so hastily shedding his sweater. The forest was getting darker and colder, shadows seeping across the floor. An irrational fear began to build inside Dr. Brown, first a coldness in the pit of his stomach, then goose bumps sprawling across his skin, the hair on the back of his neck rising . . .

Something wasn't right. He looked up at the sky, and with a stab of horror realized that he couldn't see it anymore—tendrils of shadow wove between the branches of the trees, blocking out the light. There was no cloud hiding the sun, simply a woven blanket of dark. The shadows appeared to throb, as if some unknown pulse surged within them, and with every second they grew, stretching, spiraling down the tree trunks toward the ground. Dr. Brown's heart lurched.

"Tom? Tom, if this is you doing this, it isn't funny." His voice was shaky and nearly rose into hysteria. "Tom, stop this now. I'm sorry, okay, *I'm sorry*! Call them off, whatever they are, CALL THEM OFF!"

The shadows marched on, spilling onto the forest floor all around Dr. Brown. They began lapping at his feet, and he staggered backward, stumbling away from the tree he'd been leaning against. It felt like a hundred unseen eyes were watching him, but when he spun around all he could see were trees and darkness. His breath steamed on the air.

"Tom!" screamed Dr. Brown, as the shadows rushed in to swallow him.

"TOM!"

Tea and Sympathy

THE SKY OUTSIDE THE KITCHEN WINDOW WAS DAPPLED in beautiful shades of red and orange as the sun began to creep down out of the sky. Nobody seemed to notice, though. They had other things on their minds. The policewoman sitting at the kitchen table listened carefully as Tom's mum and dad explained exactly what had happened, taking notes. In front of her on the desk lay the newspaper article that Grey Arthur had dropped.

"I found that in Tom's bedroom, just after I called you," said Tom's mum. Her eyes were surrounded with smudged mascara, and black streaks ran down her cheeks. She wiped at them with the back of her hand. "It was just on the floor. I don't know, maybe Tom had found it and tried to confront this man, or . . . I don't know, I just don't know. It was on the floor, I didn't notice it the first time I went in there, but I went back to check his room, you know, in case he'd left a note or something, just in case, and I saw it." She paused and took a deep breath. "I'm sorry, I'm babbling, I'm just worried."

"It's okay, Mrs. Golden, nothing to apologize for." The policewoman studied the newspaper article. "And you're sure this is the same man?"

"Absolutely. One hundred percent," replied Dad.

He was clutching a cup of tea, hands clinging to the warmth of the mug, but the tea itself hadn't been touched. His teeth were gritted together when he wasn't talking, and when he did speak it was in short, sharp words.

"Tom's got to be with Dr. Brown, well, no, that's not his real name, he's got to be with this *man,* and I don't know where he is, and it's our fault. We invited him into our home and . . ." Mum's voice broke then, and she couldn't say any more. She just stared into her mug, breathing deeply, shaking her head.

The policewoman nodded sympathetically, and Dad continued where Mum had left off.

"This man said he'd be able to help our son. He was very convincing, he really was. We looked him up on the computer, that's how we found him, and he seemed really genuine, and we thought we were doing the right thing, we really did. And he seemed to be making progress. Said our son was talking to some Grey Arthur, and that we needed to just leave him to it, to help out our son, so we did just that. We didn't intervene at all. But then, today, we come home and Tom's not here, I searched the neighborhood and nobody's seen him, and then we find this old newspaper article and we realize . . ." He fixed his eyes on the policewoman. They were red rimmed. "We need to find him. We need to find our son."

"He's only eleven," breathed Mum, and she

crumpled into tears, huge heavy sobs shaking her shoulders. Dad reached out and placed a hand on her, but she didn't even look up, her face buried in her hands.

"He's a young eleven," added Dad. "Maybe we shelter him a bit much, but he's an only child, and he's the youngest in his year. I mean, he's not naive, he's not daft, he knows not to go off with strangers, but this guy isn't a stranger, is he? I mean, we trusted him. We shouldn't have . . ." Dad trailed off into silence, shaking his head. "He's a young eleven. It'll be dark out there soon. Please, you have to find him."

"And we will, Mr. Golden. The police are already out there looking for him. Do you have any idea where this 'Dr. Brown' might have taken Tom?"

Dad shook his head bleakly. "We've tried phoning him back, but he's turned the phone off. He was supposed to be in a meeting, then when we phoned he said he'd hurt his ankle and didn't go, but for all we know . . ." His voice nearly broke then, heavy with frustration and fear.

"We're doing our utmost to help find your son. We just need to sit tight now and wait. You've done everything you can," said the policewoman. Mum nodded quietly, rubbing away the still falling tears as quickly as they came, but Dad got to his feet, agitated. He took the cold cups of tea from the table and poured them away down the sink.

"I can't just stay here and do nothing," he muttered, hands resting on the edge of the sink. "There's got to be something we can do."

Just then, seemingly from nowhere, a piece of paper fluttered down in the air. Slowly, gently, like a leaf falling from a tree, it tumbled down from some unknown hiding place. Dad reached out and grabbed it.

It was a scrap of paper torn from a notebook. In untidy yet clearly written letters, it said: "DUSKRIDGE WOODS."

For long seconds Dad stared at the paper, turning it in his hands, looking up to see where it could have come from. The unfamiliar writing simply stared back at him. "DUSKRIDGE WOODS."

He turned round to the policewoman, clutching the piece of paper in his hand. "Duskridge Woods!" he cried. "We have to look in Duskridge Woods!"

"What have you got there?" asked Mum. "What is it?"

"It's just a scrap of paper. I must have knocked it loose or something when I went to the sink. I don't recognize the handwriting. But it's got to be worth a try, surely?"

"It could be from anything . . . ," said Mum dismissively, sniffing back tears.

"It's worth at least checking out, surely?" he asked, looking imploringly at the policewoman. "Please."

"Okay," she said. "I'll call it through to the station.

Get some cars to go down there and have a look."

"I'm coming with you," said Dad. Mum recognized that look on his face. It was his determined look, and she knew he wouldn't give any ground.

"It's better if you stay here, Mr. Golden," said the policewoman. "Leave it to the officers."

"If he's got my son out there, then I want to be there. You can't stop me. If you won't take us, I'll drive down myself."

The policewoman paused, weighing up the situation. "We don't even know if he *is* there, Mr. Golden."

"We have to at least look. If my son *is* there . . ." He didn't need to finish his sentence. He simply looked at her, steely determination, gritted teeth, red eyes, hand clutching the scrap of paper.

"Okay," she said, nodding slowly. "Okay, I'll take you there."

"Thank you," gasped Dad. "Thank you!"

They dashed out the door, the policewoman talking into her radio, Tom's mum and dad chasing after her, scarcely pausing to shut the door behind them.

Grey Arthur stood alone in the kitchen, watching them go. He allowed himself a brief smile.

His note had worked.

Then he turned and dashed out the door, overtaking the blue flashing lights as he rushed toward Duskridge Woods.

The Grass Is Always Greener

TOM'S NOSE WAS PRESSED FLAT AGAINST THE WINDOW, and when he turned to face the Red Rascal the tip of it was smudged with dirt.

"Is it okay if I go outside and stretch my legs?"

The Red Rascal looked at him curiously. "I think they suit you that length," he replied.

"What? No! It's a phrase," said Tom, shaking his head. "I've been sitting down for too long, and I've got pins and needles. I want to walk around for a bit and get the blood flowing."

"Oh. I see!" The Red Rascal rubbed his beard. "Well, I don't see what harm it could do. Don't go too far, though—we're just here for a fleeting visit, until things get resolved back in the woods. Just long enough to teach this Dr. Brown that there's a reason why humans shouldn't try meddling with ghosts."

"What are you doing to him?" asked Tom curiously.

The Red Rascal smiled, a mischievous light in his eyes. "Let's just say that I knew some Screamers who owed me a favor. . . ."

Tom remembered then those old clicking bones, those smokey eyes, that horrible crawling fear, and he couldn't help but shudder. It was almost enough to make him feel sorry for Dr. Brown, but as he looked down at the rope marks imprinted around his wrists and thought back to everything that had happened, he soon pushed aside any fragments of sympathy. He smiled slowly at the Red Rascal.

"So I've got enough time to quickly go outside? I can't bear to be cramped up in here any longer."

"If you're quick. But don't go far!"

"Thank you!" cried Tom, already dashing out the door. "I won't be long!"

Tom stepped out in the failing light onto the perfect lawn, and it was soft and springy beneath his sock-clad feet. Everything here was perfect—each blade of grass a uniform length, each flower growing in exact rows, and not a weed in sight. The different shades of green, mowed in stripes into the lawn, look as if they had been measured to the exact millimeter. It felt a million miles away from the tangled brambles, towering stinging nettles, and strange sticky weeds of Thorbleton. The garden seemed to stretch out forever, although distantly, standing silhouetted against the multicoloured flecks of the sunset, he could see an impressive-looking building perched on the edge of the lawn. It was so far away it looked tiny, but Tom assumed that close up the building would be every inch as extravagant as the garden.

Tom wandered over to the fountain. The water tumbling down looked crystal clear, and he realized just how thirsty he was. Cupping his hands, he scooped up handfuls of water (it was deliciously cool) and drank greedily. Tom usually never drank water—he said he didn't like the taste, to which Mum would reply that it didn't have any taste, that it was just water, like air is air—but this water was actually quite nice.

Thirst quenched, Tom took the time to study his new safe haven. The bubbling fountain was dominated by a large coat of arms, a shield framed by a lion wearing a crown and a unicorn. Despite the increasing darkness, Tom could see that words ran around the edge of the shield, words in a language he couldn't understand. It looked strangely familiar, and as Tom looked down at his sock-clad feet, he hastily pulled up his trouser leg and realized that the same symbol was on his white sock. The sock that had mysteriously appeared on his bed one day.

"That's odd," he muttered to himself.

Tom wandered away from the fountain, across the striped lawn, toward the building in the distance. With every step, a tugging recognition grew. He knew this building somehow, had seen it somewhere. . . . But where? Another step, another . . . From television? From the newspapers? Another step . . . One more . . .

The Red Rascal was rummaging through Dr. Brown's belongings, trying on a red tie, when Tom flew through the door, skidding to a halt.

"The palace!" he cried, eyes wide. "We're in *Buckingham Palace*!"

"Like I said, the safest place in the whole of England. Did you enjoy your walk?" The Red Rascal was grinning, amused. Tom's mouth gaped open. "I'll take that as a yes then."

Tom sank down into the chair, shaking his head, an amazed smile on his face.

"I can't believe you took me to the palace. . . ."

"It's just as well you're back now anyway, Tom. It's time for us to head back. Are you ready? All stretched?"

Tom nodded dumbly.

"Then let's go."

You Do Not Have to Say Anything. . . .

THE POLICE CARS SPED INTO DUSKRIDGE WOODS, AND it didn't take them long to find Dr. Brown. Firstly, he was screaming so loudly that you could probably have heard him in Scotland, and secondly, when the police cars arrived, their headlights revealed him curled up in a tight ball in the middle of the clearing, rocking slightly. The Screamers had disappeared at the first sound of a police siren, and all that remained were a few shreds of shadow that clung unnaturally to the trees, when the car headlights should have chased them away. Dr. Brown hadn't seen the Screamers, but he didn't need to. Just being near to so many, feeling the chill, watching the light drain away, feeling the fear ebb from them, that had been enough. More than enough. His screams, like the shadows, were fading now, and whimpering took their place. As the police cars pulled up, he remained curled up on the ground, knees tight to his chest, eyes fixed distantly. He hadn't resisted as the police surrounded him, hadn't recoiled as the handcuffs were slammed in place, hadn't muttered a word as he was hauled to his feet. The police threw questions at him, demanding to know where Tom was, what he had done with him, but Dr. Brown just stared fixedly ahead, eyes wide, skin pale.

When he did finally speak, all he would say, over and over again, was "The ghosts were here, the ghosts were here, the ghosts were here. . . ."

The police officers exchanged worried glances.

"Split up, use your flashlights, and look around this area. If this guy's here, and his van, then Tom can't be too far away," a policewoman said, before turning her attention back to Dr. Brown. "Dr. Brown, or should I say, Gavin Snark, I am arresting you on suspicion of kidnapping. You do not have to say anything, but it may harm your defense if you do not mention when questioned something that you later rely on in court.

Anything you do say may be given in evidence. Do you understand me?"

Dr. Brown nodded silently, eyes still staring vaguely into the distance.

It was then that the police car with Tom's parents in it sped into the clearing. It braked heavily, stopping next to the other cars. Tom's mum and dad nearly fell out of the car in their haste to get out. Dr. Brown didn't even notice them arrive as he was led meekly to a waiting police car.

Tom's parents clung to each other, fingers twined together, staring at the broken mess that had once masqueraded as Dr. Brown. Dad's face was pale, his teeth gritted. Tears crowded Mum's eyes, and she desperately blinked them away. The policewoman who had driven them there approached gently, placing a hand on Mum's arm, trying to draw their eyes away from the man being shepherded away by the police.

"What happened to him?" asked Tom's mum quietly.

"We don't know, Mrs. Golden. Apparently he was like that when we arrived."

"And Tom?" asked Dad anxiously. "Where's Tom?"

"Mr. and Mrs. Golden, we'll find him. We've got lots of officers in the area, and we've every reason to believe that Tom is still in the vicinity. He can't have gone far. We *will* find him."

Mum shakily rubbed her eyes with a hand, and Dad nodded briefly.

"Keep looking," he said.

"We will, Mr. Golden," replied the policewoman, and as she walked away Dad and Mum huddled closer together.

The police car door was slammed shut, trapping Dr. Brown inside. The echo of the door slamming highlighted the silence of the woods. Police radios buzzed against a backdrop of rustling leaves.

"They'll find him," said Mum, voice small, squeezing Dad's hand. He didn't respond, he just scanned the woodland and chewed his lip, eyes distant.

The silence was unbearable.

"MUM! DAD!"

Tom's voice broke through the woods, and Mum and Dad turned round just in time to see their son crashing through the undergrowth toward them in odd socks. "Mum!" he shouted at the top of his voice. "Dad!"

Mum made a noise that might have been the beginning of a word, but that crumbled into an emotional quiver. Dad managed to find his voice, though.

"Tom!" he yelled. The family rushed together, and met in a clash of gasps, and hugs, and tears. Mum squeezed Tom so hard it felt like he might pop, and Dad just said over and over and over again, "Are you sure you're all right? Are you sure you're all right? Are you sure . . ."

"I'm fine, I'm fine," gasped Tom as he was swept up into yet another hug. Mum was crying freely, but different tears, relieved tears, and even Dad, whom Tom had never seen cry before, had tears rolling down his face. Mum held him at arm's length, studying the bruises on his hands, the dirt on his face and sleeves, before dragging him back up into another hug. Dad put his arms around the pair of them, holding both tight as if he never wanted to let go.

Just behind where Tom had dashed into the clearing, an outline of a hut could be seen in the darkness.

"I thought you said you'd searched over there?" snapped a policeman at another officer, pointing at the hut.

"I did!" the other protested. "I could have sworn I did. It wasn't there! It was just a patch of dirt!"

"Oh right, so it just appeared out of thin air, did it?" the first officer asked, one eyebrow raised. The poor policeman made some groveling excuses, but none that were believed. After all, huts don't just appear magically out of thin air. . . .

Slightly farther away, a huddle of ghosts watched the human family crying and hugging and smiling tearily at one another, before starting the process all over again.

"So, is this what being an Invisible Friend is all about then, Arthur?" asked Woeful William, dabbing his eyes with a frilly handkerchief.

Grey Arthur shrugged. "Sort of," he said. "Well, usually a little less dramatic."

So What Happened Next?

TIME SPUN ON, AS TIME DOES, NIGHT FOLLOWING DAY following night. The tears were dried away, the smiles returned, and soon everything went back to normal again—well, as normal as life can ever get with a ghost living underneath your bed.

It was "Come on, lazybones," Mr. Space Pirate cereal, Cold Fish music blaring, Dad's experimental socks, mornings with burnt toast and garish school ties, Mum's scary leftovers taking over the fridge, home-work, and lesson plans, and having to label all your pens to stop Ballpoint Bill from wandering off with them.

There was no magical happily ever after—the mornings still always came too early, the Spitting Kids still spat, Big Ben was still as big a bully as always, and Friday's lessons still dragged on for ever and ever, but somehow none of that seemed to matter as much to Tom. He had finally made some decent friends, and if they were slightly odd, or see-through, or had lopsided ears, or were prone to eating ink cartridges or forgetting to move their feet when they walk, well, these are things you can overlook.

Things did get slightly better at school, though. It's amazing what becoming a local celebrity can do. His kidnapping was headline news—the *Thorbleton Gazette* dedicated an entire front page to the story: LOCAL BOY ESCAPES CRAZED GHOST HUNTER.

Which impressed a lot of people at the school endlessly. Of course, Tom's version of events had him escaping by his wits and daring heroics, romping through the forest to freedom, and neglected to mention the intervention of a famous Poltergeist and several other ghosts, but it was probably best that way. Most humans don't believe in ghosts, after all.

Although . . .

In the police car home, exhausted and emotional, both Tom and his mum had fallen asleep, leaving Grey Arthur and Tom's dad awake. Tom's dad had removed the note from his pocket, the one with "Duskridge Woods" written on it in Grey Arthur's best handwriting, and he turned it over and over in his hands, studying it. After a while he had smilingly put it back in his pocket, and quietly, ever so quietly, whispered these words: "Thank you, Grey Arthur," before resting his head against that of his wife and falling asleep as well.

Anyway . . .

Time spun on, as time does, night following day

266

following night, and Tom Golden, Freak Boy, became Tom Golden, Local Hero, for a fleeting few weeks, until all the fuss died down. And of all the headlines in all the newspapers, he knew which one he liked the most, and which one was the truest. It was from the *Daily Tell-Tale,* and it read simply:

INVISIBLE FRIENDS SAVE THE DAY